PRAISE FOR D. ALEXANDER WARD

"D. Alexander Ward is as fine a writer as any in the field today. There's a complete confidence to his voice, teamed with an irrepressible red streak of humor, just visible beneath the horrors."

—Josh Malerman, International best-selling author of *Malorie* and *Bird Box*

"With *Beneath Ash & Bone,* Ward has created a riveting and entertainingly sinister murder mystery, full of complex characters and intriguing scenes plucked straight from our darkest nightmares."

—This is Horror Podcast

"Engaging, resonant, smart, and downright goddamn terrifying, *Beneath Ash & Bone* is a stellar achievement that transcends the genre and will leave you shaken and giddy after reading the final page. I recommend you grab this one as soon as possible and without hesitation. Truly outstanding!"

—Ronald Malfi, author of *Come With Me* and *Bone White*

"Brimming with suspense, D. Alexander Ward's excellent novel *Beneath Ash & Bone* is an eloquent—and disturbing—historic mystery with well-drawn characters and haunting imagery set in the years just before the Civil War. Horror and gothic fans, too, will be held in thrall by its dark terrors."

—Lisa Mannetti, Bram Stoker Award Winner and author of *The Box Jumper*

BENEATH ASH & BONE

D. ALEXANDER WARD

BENEATH ASH & BONE

D. ALEXANDER WARD

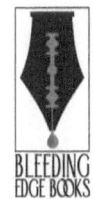

BLEEDING
EDGE BOOKS

BENEATH ASH & BONE
Copyright © 2016-2021 by D. Alexander Ward
All Rights Reserved

ISBN: 979-8218028558
Cover art by François Vaillancourt | francois-art.com
Book design & formatting by Todd Keisling | Dullington Design Co.

This is a work of fiction. Names, characters, businesses, places, events, and incidents are either the products of the authors' imaginations or used in a fictitious manner. Any resemblance to actual persons, living or dead, or actual events is purely coincidental.

No part of this publication may be reproduced, stored in a retrieval system, or transmitted in any form or by any means, without the prior permission in writing of the publisher, nor be otherwise circulated in any form of binding or cover than that in which it is published and without a similar condition including this condition being imposed on the subsequent purchaser.

Bleeding Edge Books
www.bleedingedgepub.com

*To my family and my friends,
the keepers of many's a secret.*

*"The snow doesn't give a
soft white damn whom it touches."*

—*E. E. Cummings*

BENEATH ASH & BONE

CHAPTER 1
DISAPPEARANCE

The air itself was a gale of darkness and ice that chewed into him like a storm of broken glass. Sheriff Sam Lock and his old nag of a horse, Cutter, pressed on into the bosom of a churning blizzard to find the missing boy. No more than two hours before, the sheriff had settled into a hot midnight bath when his deputy came knocking. A rider had arrived in the middle of the night with a message that a child of fourteen years had gone missing after his own birthday celebration up at the Crownhill estate: Evermore. The sprawling mansion was the home of one of Selburn's wealthiest citizens, Horace Crownhill, and his family.

Now, trotting headlong into this monster of a blizzard, that hot bath felt much more distant than just a couple of hours. Thus far, the winter of 1860 had been a hard one, so it surprised no one when the storm blew in that afternoon, kicked up its feet on Virginia's Blue Ridge Mountains and seemed content to stay awhile.

Sam raised the collar of his duster and tightened the scarf that shielded his face from the onslaught of thick flakes. Cutter had been stronger and faster in the days when his father was the head lawman in Selburn, but the old gal was showing her age tonight, slowly pressing on into the blinding white frenzy.

They crossed Foundling Creek Bridge, proceeding along a narrow trail that had vanished beneath the gathering snow. On a fair day, beyond the break in the trees, he could glimpse Evermore perched high upon the hill. But there was little hope of seeing it now. Still, he knew he was that much closer to the estate. That much closer to sheltering Cutter in the stable while he set about coordinating the search for the missing child.

As they ascended the trail, an ill wind whipped over the fields and came rushing through the break and down toward the creek. It was a peculiar stirring, whistling down the lane to confront him while the nearby trees and the snow that had gathered on them stood suddenly still. His father, who had spent his early winters near the often-snowy hills of Antrim in the north of Ireland, would have called it a white-devil wind—a movement of air borne not by nature but by the presence of something otherworldly and terrible passing through the realm of the living. He would have considered it a foreboding omen.

But Sam was not his father. That was for certain. He prided himself on being a more learned man, unchained to such old-world superstitions. It was 1860 after all, and right-thinking men had no time for such superstitions.

Cutter stalled and Sam dug his heels into the sides of the mare to spur her on but she would not be moved.

"Come on, girl." He ducked low and leaned into the wind, placing his hands on her ice-cold withers.

But Cutter was backing up, her legs unsteady in the slick snow and Sam glanced back to see them growing dangerously close to the rocky edge of the creek. He spurred her again and walloped her hind quarter but this only deepened her resolve to retreat from the oncoming wind.

"Damn it, nag," he said and tried again.

But it wasn't working and the more time he wasted trying was likely to send them both tumbling into the icy waters of the creek. He dismounted in a hurry and much to his relief, she stopped her backward movement. As he tried to steady her, she reared up and let loose a troubled moan that was lost in the screaming wind. When she came down, she whipped her heft around to catch the cold rush on her broadside but in doing so she knocked Sam to the ground where he would surely be trampled in the animal's panic.

She stood still, continuing to bellow into the oncoming wind. The wind rushed around them but the trees remained undisturbed, swaying not an inch. In that moment, it was as if the storm had ceased to exist entirely in their little part of the wood, though it filled with a gray fog that permeated the wind and brought with it an acute chill.

Cutter's ears were pinned back, reacting to something. Sam himself had the sudden sensation of being stalked, though he saw no other creatures nearby. The hair on the back of his neck stood erect as the gray mist thickened in the distance, somewhere beyond the break of the trees.

Then, just as quickly as it had set upon them, it was gone and the large flakes returned, hurling wildly through the air as the storm resumed.

Sam got to his feet and reached for the dangling reins but Cutter would have none of it. With a snort, she spun around and made for the break with speed. He took a few strides before concluding it was futile and continued up toward the break, watching her gallop away.

"Where was all that fire before?" he hollered and kicked at the snow.

Had they been farther out, he might be concerned but the old mare seemed to know where they were bound and she trotted directly up the hill toward Evermore, whose burning lanterns twinkled through the falling snow in the meager gray dawn of the coming day.

It seemed that Sheriff Sam Lock would be walking the rest of the way.

He followed the trail of Cutter's hoofmarks in the snow and after a laborious climb he crested the hill. The estate loomed before him, expansive and ornate with its walls of stone, its turrets and round spires. Practically a castle, it was far too ostentatious in its appearance even for the wealthy of Selburn. As he rounded a copse of evergreens, a dark and towering figure stepped out from behind the cascade of boughs and Sam's right hand went instinctively to the pistol at his belt, though he had the sense his reaction would have been too slow. His father had been lightning with the steel but no matter how much Sam practiced, he could never square up to his old man in that regard. Even in his position as sheriff—which he had inherited, and every soul in town knew it—he felt he was always falling short, always failing to fill those shoes.

A man's voice said, "I seen the horse and was wonderin' about the rider."

The figure carried a lantern, holding it closer to his face and Sam saw that it was one of Crownhill's servants. He relaxed his gun hand and let out a sigh.

"Shocked me there."

"Sorry 'bout that," the man said. "Ain't tryin' to get myself shot this mornin'."

"It's fine." Sam waved it off as they trudged toward the house together. "Did you happen to catch that nag?"

"Run straight for the stable. Didn't say she was called Nag, though."

"Oh?" Sam said. "Did she say she left me twisting down by the creek?"

"Sure did."

Sam laughed. "What's your name, fella?"

"They call me Colvin, sir."

As the man powered through the snow, he did so with a hitch in his step. His threadbare pants bunched up around the knee with a length of rope securing them and below that was a long iron peg ending in a brick of black metal.

"How'd you lose that leg?"

"Old master took it."

"Crownhill did that?"

"Lord, no." He winced. "Was my old master, name of Harrison who took it. Mister Crownhill give me the iron right before he cut me loose."

"You're a freed man, then?"

"Long about four years now."

"Very good." Sam gave the big man a cockeyed glance. "As for your former master, would that be Theodore Harrison?"

"Yes, sir, it would."

Sam snickered. It was Colvin's turn to raise an eyebrow of curiosity.

"Teddy Harrison, I'm told, has quite a reputation. Even among slaveholders."

Colvin grunted.

"A well-earned one, too, Sheriff."

They continued on in silence. Sam marveled at how well the man pushed through the snow with his iron peg. Colvin's old master had a penchant for cruel treatment of his slaves—far crueler than most. He was sure that Harrison had taken Colvin's leg as much for sport as he had whatever minor offense the man had committed. Crippled and devalued by his injury, Colvin was sold to the Crownhills where, at Evermore, he received fairer treatment, a new leg of sorts, and—ultimately—freedom.

And still Colvin remained in the service of the family of his own volition.

These were strange times indeed.

"I'll take you on up the house," Colvin said, breaking left for the front entrance. "Miss Charlotte's expectin' you."

They strode up the walk to the front door and Colvin opened it, ushering the sheriff inside but he did not follow.

"Colvin, how long's that boy been missing?"

The man shook his head.

"I reckon it best if you let Miss Charlotte explain." He tipped his weathered hat and shuffled away toward the far side of the property.

Sam pulled the massive front door closed. It slipped into place with a hard, metallic clack not unlike the sound of a prison cell door slamming shut.

Standing in the cavernous foyer, the sheriff called out.

"Hello?"

Hand-woven rugs from the orient covered the marble floor at the base of a grand mahogany staircase that rose up into the second level. From the outside, Sam would have guessed the estate was three stories, but looking up now, the stairway clearly ended at the second-floor balcony that looked down on the foyer.

Rows of oil lamps burned along the foyer walls. Against a corner sat a table, its legs adorned with intricate patterns that stymied the eye to discern their exact nature, though it was clearly imported from some far-off place.

Upon it sat a vase of dried flowers; white roses festooned with jasmine and lavender branches that leant to the air the fragrance of an English garden.

Other fine and ornamental trappings adorned the walls here and there but none so majestic as that above the lower landing of the staircase.

A shield emblazoned with the Crownhill family crest hung on the wall, flanked by a pair of swords whose tips pointed upward. Sam permitted himself a moment to study them and judged the blades to be far older than the Revolution. This he surmised because they had not been forged in the contemporary style. Instead, the blades were wide and pockmarked with chinks that told of battles fought in days of yore. Likely for the glory of England, for King and country, in one of its many wars. *The Hundred Years War*, he wondered? Perhaps. In any case, the swords were clearly family heirlooms and as he grazed his finger over the tempered steel, he could almost hear the guttural cries of men clothed in chainmail and plate armor. The fleshy *thwack* of limbs and heads severed from the bodies of enemies in an age where combat was always pitched, always brutal. Frenchmen had fallen under these blades, perhaps even some of his own Irish forebears.

England's legacy of brutality had a long and storied past and to proudly display such weapons in the home left Sam with the impression that nearly one hundred years prior, the Crownhills of the colonies must have been Loyalists to the crown of King George. However much he abhorred the sins of those Loyalist scum, it did not prejudice him against the living and he was no less intrigued and awed by the presence of these blades which emanated a deep and bloody history. A history the likes of which would surely never be known here in the United States.

A noise from above—a creaking board or shuffle of foot along the floor—drew his attention upward.

He cocked his head and squinted. The balcony above was shrouded in darkness but Sam thought he could make out the shape of a figure standing in its shadows. Light, perhaps, glinting off an eye. More than that, there was the sensation of being watched.

"Hello?" he called again.

Stepping forward, in the silence of the house, something crunched beneath his foot. He pulled back and bent down for a look. There, on the slick marble floor was a single black and yellow wasp, jittering and buzzing in the throes of death.

It was a curious thing to see so deep into a hard winter.

Sam was examining the odd thing so intently that he didn't even notice the gentle footsteps of the woman as she approached him from the parlor.

"Deputy?"

Sam turned and beheld what might have been the finest thing he had ever seen in all of God's creation. She had long, blond locks of hair that wept down the sides of her porcelain face and ended in a cluster of curls just below her shoulders. She wore a simple, cotton house dress and a worried expression.

"Sheriff, actually," he said, though he instantly felt foolish for doing so. "Ma'am?"

"I'm Charlotte Crownhill."

"Yes, ma'am," he said, getting straight to the matter at hand. "I understand that there is a missing child?"

"Two missing."

"Two?" Sam said. "The boy..."

"My nephew, William." Her eyes welled up with tears. "And the girl that went looking for him."

"A girl? Why was she allowed to go mucking around in this storm?"

But he had his answer in the sudden quiver of her lips.

"Please tell me about the girl."

She choked back something deep and she choked it back hard.

"Her name is Lucy," she said, her voice breaking. "She's my daughter."

Sam nodded as the woman wiped tears from her stark blue eyes.

"She is aged fourteen, the same as William. I'm afraid she hasn't been seen since this morning after we realized that he was missing. She is quite fond of her older cousin."

"What of the boy's parents?"

"Mister and Missus Blake are traveling," she said. "Europe, I think, or perhaps Asia."

Sam removed a small, leather-bound book and pencil, scribbled notes and names.

"You have to find them, Sheriff. You *have to*."

He started to utter promises about how the children would be safe and sound when they found them and how tomorrow they would all be laughing about the whole affair. It would have assuaged her worry, no doubt, but such promises would be empty.

"I'll find them," he said instead, with some determination. "Miss Crownhill, I will find them."

She blubbered her thanks to him. He nodded, walked to the window and stared out the front of the house.

"If we're going to do this, though," he turned and said to her as gently as possible. "I'll need help. Volunteers. Men who hunt and know this country."

"We've arranged for that, Sheriff. You need only look out back."

Sam followed her through the foyer and dining room into the kitchen, where she threw open the rear door to the house. To his surprise, an army of country folk stood at the ready, torches and lanterns burning, looking very much like a lynch mob.

"Very good." He closed the door. "I'll need a map of the property. Something showing the geographic features, notable places around the estate. Every nook and cranny."

"I thought you might." She produced a sheaf of rolled paper. "I found this in the secretary."

He unrolled it and glanced at it, nodding with approval.

"If there's anything missing from the map, Colvin can direct you to it," she said further. "No one knows this place as well as him."

"Mister Crownhill...is your husband?"

She regarded him curiously. "He is my father."

Well, he had certainly stepped in it, hadn't he? "You're not married, then?"

She shook her head. "Widowed, actually. I'm afraid that Neville succumbed to consumption some years ago."

"My apologies," he offered. "With the urgent nature of the case, I had no time to familiarize myself with the details of your family. Though I'm not sure I would have discovered much. Your father is reputed to be an intensely private man."

She scoffed.

"You have no idea, Sheriff. You really don't."

"And where is Mister Crownhill? I suppose I should let him know I've arrived."

"Father is away in Richmond, Sheriff. On business."

"I see."

He slid the map into his inner coat pocket and smoothed his duster. "Yes, well...we should begin. It'll be light soon and I'd like for the search to be well underway by then."

She nodded and opened the door for him. "Thank you, Sheriff," she said as he descended the rear steps.

Sam turned and tipped his hat to her before striding down into the crowd and barking orders. But even as he did so, his mind kept returning to Charlotte Crownhill's porcelain skin, so uniquely perfumed and smelling more of rosewater and lilacs than any woman had a right to in the middle of a winter storm.

The morning sky was a pale, gray blanket from which snow continued to fall, accumulating quickly. Time was running out and though he spoke nothing of it, Sam grew increasingly doubtful about the prospect of finding the boy alive if he had become lost out in the wild—but there was still hope for the girl if they could get to her soon enough.

He directed the volunteers to split into three groups to search the east, west and north quadrants of the property. He kept Colvin with him so that he would have the man's knowledge of the house and grounds at his disposal. They, along with four others, searched the eastern portion where the woods were the thickest. Out this way there were also the overgrown and long disused fields from a time when the estate had been a proper farming operation. Scattered about were the ramshackle buildings where the slaves who had worked them were once quartered.

As he learned from talking with Colvin, though, Horace Crownhill had shut the farm down to pursue filling his coffers by way of a trade business, importing and exporting goods to and from England and other more exotic places overseas. It certainly explained the eclectic collection of goods and decorations carefully placed throughout the home. Around the same time, the Crownhill patriarch had freed or sold his slaves. Those who remained—Colvin, his mother, Seena, his niece, Mary and a pair of nephews who were young men in their own right—lived there on the estate in newer quarters. They now upheld their duties of maintaining the home and grounds, and as payment they received food and shelter as well as a monthly wage from the Crownhills.

When Sam asked why the nephews hadn't joined in the search party, the big man said it was their preference to keep out of Crownhill family business. That and they were concerned about being left alone with some of the other volunteers, white folk who might have a mind to harm or kill them for sport, even in the midst of the search. Having seen the rabble that made up the search party, Sam did not think the nephews' concern unfounded.

"Since you're free, why wouldn't you and the others go north?" Sam asked as they walked the thick wood in the gray light, searching for any sign of passage.

"Don't know anybody up north," the man said. "'Sides, Momma wouldn't live through it. Too far to go."

"What was it that made the old man close down the farm and let y'all go?"

The big man shrugged.

"Some folks say he ain't well."

"Oh?"

"Touched in the head, they say."

"Really? Who says that?"

But Colvin just smiled.

"Folks."

He was tight as a clam, the big man was, and seemed quite loyal to the Crownhills—an admirable trait. Or perhaps it was more about survival. Life for freed men outside of the plantations was hard going, even far to the north.

They were picking through a deep drift of snow that had gathered on an embankment when a hollering came from behind them. Sam turned to see a young man slogging his way through the shin-deep snow toward the edge of the wood and he went to meet him.

"What is it?"

"The girl," the lad said hoarsely, gasping for breath. "They've found the girl. She's going to be okay. Taking her back to the house now."

There, at least, was some victory.

"Where did they find her?"

"In the hollow of an old tree. Down by the pond."

Sam unrolled the paper and scanned it but after a moment his face tightened in some places and wrinkled in others with anger. He shook his head and pounded a fist onto the paper.

"That ain't on the map," he growled, then turned to Colvin who was trudging toward them as best he could, dragging his iron peg through the snow.

He held out the paper to the big man.

"The pond where they found the girl ain't on this map. I need you to look and tell me what else ain't on this goddamned map!"

Sam and Colvin huddled behind a broad chestnut tree to get out of the wind and the sheriff pressed the map against it while the big man used Sam's pencil to mark other missing features. Sam watched as he did so, asking about this place or that. Colvin drew a cross onto the map at a point deep into the southern reaches of the eastern wood.

"And that?" he asked.

"That's where the old tobacco barn was."

Back when Evermore had been a working plantation, that building was where they would have taken the chopped tobacco and hung it to cure. Sam chewed it over for a moment.

"What's out there now?"

"Ain't nothin' out there now."

"The barn's been torn down, has it?"

The big man snorted.

"More like fell down. There's some of it left. Ain't no better than a pile of sticks, though."

Sam nodded.

"Anything else out there?"

"Old farming works. Ox harnesses, reapers, busted wagons."

Sam could feel Colvin watching him as the wheels turned in his mind.

"The children know not to play out there, Sheriff."

Sam snatched the map from the tree and rolled it up.

"Of course they do," he said with pointed sarcasm. "And it's well known that children never play where they're told not to."

"Pardon?"

"Come on," Sam said, a sharp edge in his voice. "We need to search there."

During the first few hours of the storm, the forest floor—thick with towering pines and scrubby evergreens—had accumulated less snow than the open areas so the going was easier there. Even so, Sam and the big man trudged through drifts that had gathered against thickets and in shallow ravines that sometimes plunged them waist-deep into the white. Finally, up ahead Sam saw the tobacco barn.

He learned from Colvin that another plantation had once stood on the property. But it had burnt down half a century before Horace Crownhill came along and acquired the land, building Evermore over top the ashes of the old place.

Some of the old buildings, such as the tobacco barn, were all that remained.

What this land had been called back in those days, Colvin could not say. He could only offer that in his time at Evermore, other slaves spoke of the place in careful whispers. Some said that its soil had seen more blood than any place should, long before even the first white settler got the notion to lay a foundation there. The tribe of Monacan Indians who once called it home had warred with other tribes and even themselves for decades. Those same tribesmen were slaughtered by English settlers when they ventured deeper into the New World. Many years later, those loyalist settlers were killed in turn by American revolutionaries. Not long after, a nearby village of mixed-race Melungeons were run off with intimidation and murder by white purists who came to power in Selburn in the early years of the republic. It seemed that at one time or another, folk were always murdering someone else to possess this place for their own.

As they entered the clearing, Sam saw that the barn was as the big man had described it—a leaning shelter of old boards and beams that had mostly fallen in on itself long ago. But there was some structure left to it, however precarious it might have been, and it could still afford a small measure of shelter to someone desperate enough.

"William!" Sam cried out as he approached it. "Can you hear us, boy? Are you there?"

There was no reply, no noise at all save for the wind and the rustle of snowflakes piling upon snowflakes.

Sam entered the remains of the structure and scanned it for signs of recent passage or habitation, but if someone had spent any time in this place, it was not plain to see and certainly not since the storm had begun. The innards of the structure were undisturbed and upon every surface exposed to the elements, there was a uniform gathering of white.

Sam's heart sank. Until that moment, even he himself had not known how much he hoped they would find the boy there. After seeing Colvin scrawl it onto the map, he had a simple and powerful hunch that the old barn would bear some fruit in their search. But it was no more than another lonely, deserted place in the wood, forgotten by all but time itself, which had whittled it down to almost nothing.

The sheriff leaned against a fallen, rotting timber that bent with his weight but did not break. He breathed a heavy sigh. Even so many years later, there was the lingering aroma of the thousands of pounds of tobacco that had passed through it. Looking to the north, deeper into the wood, though, his heart leaped in his chest as something formed in the snowy wind—a shape, tall as a man, shrouded and unclear in the blowing white.

"Hey!" he said as he and plodded through the ruin of the barn to the other side, boards splintering beneath his strides and the whole thing groaning with complaint, ready to complete its slow death at any moment.

He could hear the shouts of the big man urging him not to go any farther but Sam powered on and when he came out on the other side of the barn, he continued toward the blurry shape a dozen yards away.

"Stay where you are, William," he shouted, frantic to reach the boy.

His strides sank deep into the snow, some deeper than others, and it was plain that he was traversing not flat, open ground but a field of debris whose many crevices had been filled with snow.

"Almost there," he said, breathless, just before the ground beneath him gave way and he plunged down into a hard, sharp thing that tore a long gash in his leg.

Sam wiggled free of the hole and continued, heedless of the pain, but when he looked up to the figure in the wind, it was gone. Still, he would not be deterred. Out of the corner of his eye, he saw Colvin, carefully picking his way among the snow covered debris and begging him to come off of it.

When the sheriff reached the spot where the figure had been, there was nothing. No William, no footprints in the snow. Not even the wisp of a narrow sapling pine that might account for what he saw.

But he *had seen something*.

"Here," he mumbled with labored breath. "He was right here."

Confronted with this barren patch, Sam went slack and found himself in snow all the way to his knees as he bowed his head and pitched forward. As his gloved hands drove downward through the cold, they touched something. Something that did not belong in this place.

"Sheriff, why don't you back out of there now? Real slow and easy afore you get yourself hurt bad."

Sam Lock heard the big man but he paid no mind. He was digging.

"There's something," he shouted. "Something here."

When the fingers of Sam's leather gloves got thick with so much of the frozen stuff as to be useless, he tore them off and dug with his bare hands.

"Sheriff, please."

He dug until his hands were ice and when they were ice, he dug until they were raw; until he uncovered what some grim part of him knew was there beneath the white.

The smooth face of a young man, wide-eyed with terror, lay frozen there in the snow. As he brushed ice and snow away from William's face, he at last gave out and slumped backward, his chest heaving in the chill air.

"Lord God," he heard Colvin say in a trembling whisper.

They both sat there for a long moment, neither man uttering a word. The snow continued to fall and the wind to blow, unimpressed by this awful discovery.

Sam sat up and began to dig away the snow from the body.

"Call them," he said to Colvin. "Call them all. Tell them we found the boy."

The big man looked on for a moment.

"What you doin', Sheriff? That boy's dead."

Sam was heaving a handful of snow from around where he figured William's shoulders to be.

"I know he's dead, Colvin," he said. "Now I need to know how he got to be that way."

The big man hesitated.

"Go," Sam urged. "Go and get the others."

"This ground ain't safe, Sheriff."

Sam nodded.

"I know. Go and get them. Please."

He continued to dig and as the big man went down into the wood he heard him mutter under his breath.

"Reckless," Colvin said and shook his head.

Sam Lock snorted but kept on. After all, it wasn't the first time he had been called such.

CHAPTER 2
DISCOVERIES

By the time the other volunteers came, Sam had managed to clear most of the snow away from the boy's torso and as the men gathered close by, stepping across the precarious ground, the sheriff cleared away a layer of icy white from the boy's chest, giving them all a good look at what had been his undoing. A wide, red bloom radiated outward away from a single metal blade that poked upward through the boy's chest from beneath him. The volunteers explained to the sheriff that judging from the visible debris in the area, somewhere underneath the snow was the wreckage of an old reaping machine. Pulled by a team of horses, the machine was designed to harvest wheat and other small grains. This one had disintegrated many years ago and its metal pieces lay apart from each other, though the right-angle bracket that held the machine's cutting blade had fallen in such a way that it left the blade pointing skyward, a hazard of the most dire sort.

Sam listened as, under their breath, the volunteers mumbled and shook their heads at the senselessness of it. Lost in the storm, the boy had perhaps sought the shelter of the dilapidated barn but had picked the worst route to approach it. With the ground covered in snow, he wouldn't have seen the dangers beneath. Just as Sam hadn't when he went tramping out of the barn toward that gray shape he had seen...or thought he had seen.

It was all just bitter, bad luck. Sam had managed it, sustaining only a flesh wound while the boy, William must have slipped, lost his footing and fallen backward, impaling himself on the wicked blade of the old machine.

William died where he fell, Sam reckoned, his cries—if he had given any—unheard and unanswered even as so many others fretted over his absence. To this bleak end, the mystery of the missing child was now solved.

Sam stood to address the volunteers.

"Gentlemen, I thank you for your time and your considerable effort. It's now a matter for the police and the family, though. Go on back to your homes and the warmth of your hearths."

The lot of them shuffled away, leaving only Colvin still standing where the others had gathered. Sam saw that he carried a bundle beneath one arm and a few tall wooden poles in his hand.

"What's all that?" he asked.

"For shelter," Colvin said. "Reckoned it might help keep the snow off us while we dig him out."

Sam nodded. It was good thinking.

"When we're done, we can use it for a shroud to carry him out of here," Colvin added.

"Yeah, all right."

The sheriff took a couple of the poles and began to help the big man erect a makeshift shelter over the body. As they worked getting the poles upright in the snow and the canvas tarpaulin stretched across them, Colvin's gaze constantly drifted to the body and the red bloom that radiated outward from the fatal wound.

"Never seen a dead body?" Sam asked.

The big man shook his head. "Not like this, I ain't."

"Well, then you and I have more in common than you might think."

Sam had seen his share of dead bodies and, in the line of duty, had produced some of them himself—but never a child and never in such awful circumstances as these.

As they finished the shelter, Sam got back onto his knees in the snow and continued to unearth the body. Digging around the perimeter of the boy's corpse, he hoped that if they could clear the top and sides, they might be able to lift him out.

As he scooped snow away from the boy's knees, he happened upon a curious sight—bare flesh. The boy's skin was darker and discolored, presumably from exposure, the life long since drained from it. The paleness of death was upon it, the kneecap staring up at him from the ice and snow. He scraped more away to see the upper leg, also bare. It almost seemed as if the child had been pantless when he met his end. But what sense did that make?

Sam continued to unearth the lower half of the boy, scooping and scraping, finding every bit of his lower legs to be naked flesh. Even more peculiar, when he got to the boy's feet and ankles, he found the bunched up cloth of the boy's trousers around them.

"I don't understand," he said.

Colvin, who had been lingering in the back, smoking on a tobacco pipe, shrugged.

"Answerin' nature's call, I reckon."

"Right," the sheriff said, thinking it over. "I suppose."

Lost, alone in the dark and the wild, frightened. It seemed a hell of a time to relieve oneself.

Sam leaned over to scoop from the far side of the body and beneath his knees the snow shifted. He pitched forward, putting an arm out to steady himself and as his hand dug into the snow over the boy's waist and slipped, it revealed another red bloom in the white.

"What the hell?" Sam muttered as he righted himself, looking over the body.

He reached down and brushed more of the snow away from the boy's waist and the deeper he went, the more snow came away blood red.

Now, bent over the body and frantically scraping and tossing snow away, it was only a moment before he uncovered the boy's naked waist and what he found there shocked him to the core. So badly that he turned and retched the meager contents of his guts out into the snow behind him.

"You all right, Sheriff?"

"Am I *all right?*" he scoffed, spitting chunks.

His head was on fire, his thoughts racing. Colvin sure had tried to pull

Sam away from digging in the snow. Pleaded with him to give up and move on. As if he had known what lay under that snow. And now, Sam couldn't help but wonder why the big man was not similarly sickened at the sight of what was being uncovered, but when he looked over at his face, he could see that was not entirely true. Colvin's lip was curled up, baring his yellowed teeth and his eyes were averted from the boy's mangled genitals.

"You reckon an animal been scavengin' at him?" Colvin asked, his face looking pained as he struggled to keep the gorge down in his throat.

Sam looked over the body again, this time with a deliberate effort not to vomit. It was possible. Hell, it was more than possible. It was likely. So what was it that gave the sheriff pause?

"No more digging on the waist," Sam said. "Help me dig around him and let's get this boy out of the snow."

"Yes, sir," Colvin said, sinking to his knees on the side opposite the sheriff and scooping the snow away.

"One more thing," the sheriff said.

"What's that?"

"When we carry the boy back to the house, no one gets a look at him until I say so. Understand?"

Colvin nodded.

"And tell no one about the boy's...private bits. Not until I've had time for a closer examination."

"Yes, sir."

At the sheriff's careful direction, they cleared William's body and pried him from the snow with some effort, so frozen was he there in the white. All the while, Sam wondered what it was, niggling at the back of his mind, that kept him from declaring the boy's death a simple and unfortunate accident.

That was the problem with lawmen, though. They had a troublesome knack for knowing when something just didn't track.

As they carried the boy's frozen body through the east wood toward the Crownhill manor house, the more he thought on it, the more insistent that scratching at his mind became. It might well have been an animal, scavenging the soft tissue of the boy's body for food. But the profound rigidity of the body when they went to move him spurred another notion that the sheriff could not shake. The corpse was so frozen through that it didn't seem possible it had gotten that way in just the few hours since the storm began the previous afternoon. Which meant that William had been out in the east wood by the old barn the night before while everyone else was in the Crownhill home celebrating his birthday.

So what was the young lad doing so far from the festivities, alone, relieving himself among a field of lethal old farm equipment, with his goddamned trousers around his ankles?

Back at the house, Charlotte took William's demise hard. After Sam broke the news to her that he had fallen, the apparent victim of an accident over by the old tobacco barn, she sank down into the couch with her head in her hands and wept as he stood there, awkwardly twiddling his fingers to the notes of an old reel his father used to play.

"Can I see him?" she asked.

The sheriff shook his head.

"I need to examine the body further," he said.

"Why is that?"

"I assure you that it's just procedure in such matters. Things that must be done to close the case, ma'am."

She sniffled and nodded.

"You'll return to do that, then, when the storm has passed?"

"I'm afraid not, Miss Charlotte. I'll need to remain with the body until my examination and report is complete."

It would have been his preference to transport the corpse back to Selburn where he and the local mortician could conduct their inspection, but the weather prohibited such a journey at the moment.

"I see," she said. "You'll need a place to stay, then."

"If it wouldn't be too much trouble."

"Of course," she said, standing, affecting a cheerful air. "We'd be glad to have you. There's a guest house out back where my father stayed for a time. It's vacant now but I could have the servants ready it for you if you like."

"Sounds just fine."

"Would you take tea, Sheriff?" she asked, though she glanced over to a glass decanter on a nearby table. "Or would you prefer something stronger?"

"Stronger sounds good," he replied.

A glass of whiskey or brandy would do much to banish the cold that had seeped deep down into his aching bones.

She poured and handed him a glass.

"How is your daughter, ma'am?"

She sighed, her countenance heavy with the family's troubles.

"Fragile," she said. "I fear that she will not take this news well."

He nodded as he sipped the whiskey.

Then, without warning, there came the sound of a young woman's voice.

"What news, Mother?"

Sam turned to see a young girl standing at the opening of the parlor. From her blue eyes and golden hair, it was plain to Sam that this was Charlotte's daughter, Lucy. She stood nearly as tall as her mother, though she bore the physical awkwardness of a growing adolescent. She had a blanket wrapped around her and her skin was pale, her long locks still drying from the clinging snow.

"Lucy?" Charlotte gasped, going to her daughter's side and drawing the blanket tighter around the girl. "What are you doing out of bed?"

The girl shrugged, pushing herself away from her mother as the woman tried to hold her in an embrace.

"I couldn't sleep," she said, annoyed. "Who is he? And what news?"

Charlotte cast a labored glance toward Sam, expectant.

"Lucy, my name is Sheriff Lock and..."

"Your first name is Sheriff?"

Sam grinned, knowing that this was not so much a question as it was a snide and impolite criticism of his authority. *Ah, youth.*

"Lucy!" Charlotte exclaimed, her eyes wide and disapproving.

"My first name is Samuel," he said. "But you can call me Sam if you like."

He looked to Charlotte for further explanation but she adopted the steady, downward stare of a beaten parent, leaving the rest up to him.

Very well, then.

"Your cousin, William, is gone," he uttered. "It appears there was an accident and the wound he sustained was mortal."

"He died?" Lucy asked as her knees trembled and she went down upon them.

"I am sorry for your loss, miss."

But Lucy didn't hear him. She was lost in her grief, sobbing into Charlotte's arms.

The woman cast a glance at Sam, at his haggard appearance and trousers wet beyond the knees.

"Father is a much slighter man," Charlotte said. "But you could fit into his clothes. He has closets of them that he no longer wears."

Sam stared down at his own wretchedness.

"I do appreciate it, ma'am."

Cradling her sobbing daughter, Charlotte waved it off.

"It's the least I can do."

She shouted then for someone named Bet and a moment later, a young servant that must have been one of Colvin's nephews appeared. Easily sixteen years of age, Bet was a tall and stocky lad with cherubic features and a careful, serious demeanor that reminded Sam very much of the boy's uncle.

"Ma'am?"

"Take Sheriff Lock and show him to Father's room, please. He's in need of some clothes and should have no trouble finding something there."

"Yes, ma'am."

Sam nodded at Charlotte and followed Bet out into the foyer. As they ascended the staircase, he could still hear the sobs of young Lucy as her mother held her close, straining to comfort her.

Bet led the sheriff up the stairs to the landing on the second floor balcony. The finery of the home continued there as well with floors of polished marble upon which stood a crescent table so ornate it could only have been imported from somewhere in Europe. On the walls hung a handful of paintings; mostly of landscapes not unlike those around Selburn itself. Several rooms stood off the wide hallway. One door was wide open, which he presumed to be Lucy's room, as the sheets on the bed looked freshly disturbed.

He followed as Bet turned to the right and opened two double doors into the master suite. Hanging on the wall outside of the room, Sam noticed a weathered map of the southern territories near Mexico and Texas and next to it a Colt pistol mounted to a plaque with an inscription that read, *Sergeant Horace M. Crownhill, 1847-1848.*

Pausing, he inspected it closely. Dust had been allowed to collect on it but the weapon itself had been well used in its day and even now, he thought he could see the gleam of live rounds in the chamber. Horace, it seemed, had once served in the Army and judging from the years on the inscription, it would have been during the war with Mexico that had ended over a decade ago. From the notches scratched into the grip, Sam judged that the patriarch had put many a *soldado* in the ground with the Colt.

The servant boy cleared his throat, waiting beside the open doors and Sam nodded as he came along.

"Sorry," he offered. "I'm fascinated by all things military."

"Yes, sir."

Bet stood by the door of Horace Crownhill's bedchamber as Sam perused the patriarch's extensive wardrobe. The vast majority were the clothes of a gentleman and much more formal than the sheriff had need of. But farther in the back of the enormous closet, he did find some outdoor clothing that seemed to have been worn for hunting.

"Bet?"

"Yes, sir?"

"Mister Crownhill has a good deal of hunting clothes and gear in here. Was he much of an outdoorsman?"

"He could hunt a deer as well as any. Didn't go very often. Uncle says that after he come home from the war, he was always more of the indoor sort. And now…"

The young man drifted off and Sam stuck his head out from the closet.

"Yes?" he asked. "What sort is he now?"

Bet sighed, looked down to the floor.

"I can't rightly say."

Sam's eyes narrowed.

"You know, Bet, whenever Mister Crownhill is brought up in conversation, the folk around here seem rather loathe to discuss the master of the house. Why is that?"

Bet shrugged.

"You gonna have to ask Miss Charlotte about that, Sheriff."

Sam returned to the closet, disrobing and picking a fresh pair of trousers and a heavier coat from among the many available.

"Yes," he said. "I suppose I will. All in due time."

When he was done dressing in the borrowed clothes, he returned to the bedchamber.

"I can take you back to the parlor if you like, sir. Or maybe out to the guest house?" Bet asked.

"I've been meaning to ask about that as well. It's rather unusual to have such accommodations for guests outside of the main house, ain't it?"

The boy shrugged.

"Mister Crownhill had it built for himself. Back before he got sick."

"I see. For privacy, then?"

Bet nodded.

"Just how sick is Mister Crownhill?"

He shrugged.

"He must be well enough to be away on business, though. Williamsburg, isn't it?"

"Yes, sir. Williamsburg."

Having caught the boy in a lie, Sam smiled.

"Another point of inquiry for Miss Charlotte, I suppose."

"Yes, sir," Bet said and led him out of the room and down the main stairs. "I can take you there now if you like."

"Not necessary. I'd like to see your quarters."

"Pardon?" the boy said, his pace slowing.

"I have an arrangement with your uncle, Colvin."

"All right."

Dusk had turned to night by the time they stepped out of the manor house and were enveloped at once in the churning blizzard. There was a wide swath of open ground to cross before they could reach the servants' quarters. As they trudged through the white, Sam stopped.

"Wait," he hollered, not knowing if his voice was lost in the wind.

He reached out, grabbed the young man's shoulder and turned him around.

"Sir?" the boy replied, squinting his eyes against the frozen wind.

"Why do they call you 'Bet?'" he asked. "Is it short for something?"

The young man scoffed, then smiled. "It ain't short for nothin', no."

Sam remained there in the blistering gale, his hand on the boy's shoulder and when Bet saw that he wouldn't be put off, he explained.

"Uncle Colvin says when I's born, I won't no bigger than a half-eaten loaf of bread. Skinny as a picked chicken. Most of the folks took up a wager that I wouldn't make it through the night. Wasn't much a wager, though, since most of 'em agreed. And when I come through it, they sweetened the pot for the next night and the night after that, and so on. I lived all them days and more, so they named me Bet."

"What'd your uncle say when they were betting on your life?"

"Way I heard it told, Uncle Colvin never wagered. Said he knew I's gonna make it."

Sam grinned.

"And now you're almost as big as your uncle. I reckon you showed the others."

"You reckon right," Bet said, then made to move on, but stopped and turned to face him.

"Sheriff, mind if I ask why you asked that?"

A razor wind blew in from the west and Sam grimaced against it.

"I just like to know who's leading me through the dark, son," he said. "Carry on."

As they got closer, Sam could just barely make out the servants' housing through the blinding swirl of snow and ice. It was, of course, a modest structure with no perceptible windows. All the same, he detected slivers of light burning inside, the rays slipping out through the narrow gaps in the boards which defended the quarters against the elements. On a night such as this, though, Sam thought with some disdain, the thin boards of its outer walls surely did not afford the dwellers much comfort from the cold. A plume of smoke rose from the chimney, although in the searing wind he could not see it so much as smell its odor of burning logs. The pungent scent of hickory and gum, the sweetness of pine.

As the two of them stumbled in, slamming the door shut behind them, Sam found the others gathered at a table too long for their number, reclining away from their empty plates and engaged in quiet conversation. The common area was clean and perfectly serviceable, though Sam imagined that it had once been host to many more bodies than were present. There was a small kitchen off to the side. Sconces with burning candles on the barren white walls lit the room well.

As Sam stepped in and removed his hat, Colvin pushed back in his chair and stood.

"Evening, Sheriff. Make you some supper?"

"Thank you, but no," Sam said.

Colvin motioned to the others. "This is my family."

He introduced them all in turn. Bet, of course, he had already met. His brother, Twig, was the opposite image of the hefty young man, though, short in stature and thin as a reed. There was little to guess regarding how his name had come to him. About the same age as Bet and just as quiet and purposeful, his complexion was darker and his hair longer and wilder upon his head. Colvin's niece by a sister who had long ago been sold off, Mary was a strikingly beautiful colored girl with long, black hair pulled back into braids and wide, doe eyes that aligned with high, sculpted cheekbones. Though to call her a girl was not exactly true. She had the look of a young woman in her twenties. When he was introduced to her, Mary returned a cordial smile so infectious the sheriff could not help but grin in return despite the grim circumstances of their meeting.

When Colvin introduced his mother, a positively ancient looking woman called Seena, she did not stand to greet him. Instead, she looked down at a carved wooden platter on the table before her that was filled with sand. Upon the sand, she had traced lines with her fingers. Her hands came up from under the table and she emptied them in a gentle throw over the platter. What must have been about two dozen acorns scattered across the wooden dish and came to rest, carving new designs into the sand. She gave Colvin an approving nod.

Seena then stood, as well as she was able, her back having long ago twisted to bend her forward in a permanent lean, but her arms looked taut and strong enough from what Sam supposed had been a lifetime of hard labor. She offered the sheriff a smile and a nod.

"Pleased to meet you, Sheriff."

"Likewise," he said.

But for all her warmth, Sam found his eyes returning to the wooden platter and the acorns. As well, he found her gaze upon him a little unsettling—as if she were not looking *at him* so much as *into him*.

"Well," Colvin said, "me and the sheriff got some business to take care of. Y'all go on up the house. Make sure Miss Charlotte and Miss Lucy doin' all right."

With that, the others filed out of the building to trudge across the snowy yard. For a moment, the two men stood in silence.

"Sure I can't fix you somethin' to eat?" the big man asked.

"No. And it's probably best that you ate first," the sheriff remarked. "I'm afraid that after what comes next, neither of us may have much of an appetite left."

Colvin nodded and they both walked past the roaring fire to a door that opened into a storeroom. Before stepping out of the common room, Sam felt his eyes drawn back to the platter and the acorns on the table.

"Mama was castin' the Ifá," Colvin said, following his stare.

"That like telling fortunes?"

Colvin shifted. "Somethin' like that. Mama always use Ifá for guidance."

"Well," the sheriff said, "I reckon we could all use more of that."

The room being adjacent to where the servants ate, on the left wall was the brick and stone of the fireplace chimney, which had not been kept up to snuff and breathed a great deal of its heat into the room. Colvin and Bet had placed the boy's body there—so that it might have a chance to thaw for the examination.

Scattered among the bags of grain and flour, he saw bedding. All of them on the floor, save for one in the corner, raised up on sticks with a battered mattress. It was a comfort that Sam assumed was afforded to the old woman, the matriarch of their family. They slept here during the cold months, he realized. Even with the rats and other vermin so attracted to the stores, they slept here nonetheless for the warmth radiating from the fireplace chimney.

The body lay on a cot nearby, still covered in the canvas tarpaulin and Sam could see Colvin regarding it with no small amount of dread.

"Don't worry," Sam offered. "I'll keep your assistance to a minimum if at all possible."

"I sure thank you for that."

He uncovered William and prodded the flesh of his belly to find it softened. The body had thawed well and the fatal wounds on his chest were reddened with the trauma of their making. The residual snow and ice on the body had melted and pooled red on the floor, seeping down into the floorboards and the space beneath.

Now unfrozen, the boy's genitals were even more ghastly to behold than before. Reluctantly, Sam plucked at the tissue. However this had been done, with whatever sort of blade, there had been long, vertical lacerations up and down the length of the boy's member, shredding into several pieces what had once been whole, though they were all still attached at the base.

"A clear bottle, filled with water, please." He looked to Colvin.

After a moment, the big man returned and handed Sam a tall bottle once filled with liquor but now heaping with water. He plunged his thumb into the neck of it to serve as a cork and then tipped the bottle over, holding it close to the wounds, magnifying their image through the bottle.

"This wasn't the work of an animal," he said aloud, talking mostly to himself. "If it were, I'd expect to find the edges of these lacerations to be rough. Flesh chewed away. But these are smooth—definitely the work of some kind of blade, something very sharp."

"Dear Lord," the big man moaned and sat down behind him.

Sam set the bottle down on the floor and covered the body.

"The chest wound is what killed him," Sam continued. "Maybe it was an accident and maybe it wasn't. But whatever else was done to this child, *this* injury was very sinister and very intentional."

Colvin hung his head.

"Any ideas on who might have done this?" Sam asked.

"Not at all," the big man said. "No one I can think of."

"Perhaps some of the neighboring folk who had a problem with the boy?"

"He's just a child, Sheriff. What kind of grown man has a problem with a child that would make him do such a thing?"

It was a vexing question to be sure. Sam thought of what Colvin had told him about the reputation of this place—how so much blood had been spilled upon it over the centuries, as if the land itself, every now and then, grew hungry. And if that were true, then this being the first untimely death visited upon the Crownhill family was something of a wonder.

"Sheriff, you all right?"

Sam must have had a faraway look about him. He nodded and blinked the thoughts from his head. That was his old culchie bogman of a father talking, not him. The idea of the land being cursed was baseless superstition and nothing more.

"Listen," he said. "What we have seen stays between you and me. But there's no need for William to remain in here. He'll only begin to smell. Wrap him up tonight and move him outside. Bury him in snow. That'll preserve him for now."

Colvin rubbed over the thick stubble of his face and nodded.

"Will do, sir."

"I'll be interviewing the family tomorrow. Someone must have some idea of what might have happened here and who might have done this."

"Yes, sir."

Sam pulled on his coat and left the servants' quarters for the small guest house at the rear of the property. He stopped at the back of the manor house and rapped on the kitchen door so that Bet could escort him to the guest house.

There was most certainly someone who had had a very serious problem with the boy and, though Colvin claimed he could not imagine why, it was not difficult for Sam to do so. He said nothing of it during the examination but the first thing he noticed after uncovering the boy's body in the store room, thawed and with the pale sheen of ice melted from his flesh was the curiously dark and curly hair upon his head. William was not white—not entirely. Sam had known many Melungeons in his time, especially in these parts of Virginia; those who had been bred of Indians and Negroes, whites and dark-skinned foreigners such as Spaniards and Italians. But Sam's well-educated guess was that the boy, William, was simply half white and half Negro.

And a half-breed living in the family home, treated and educated as though he were of "pure" blood? That was something that would never have sat well with the folk in these parts. Not well at all.

CHAPTER 3
NIGHT VISITORS

The guest house was situated nearly as far away from the manor house as were the servants' quarters. It had been constructed at the bottom of a hill that sloped away from the house and overlooked a shallow run of water that, Sam had no doubt, would be the picture of tranquility in spring and summer. Its babbling flow among the mountain rocks would lull even the most anxious of guests into a deep and abiding slumber.

But it was winter and the run was frozen solid.

The abode itself was made entirely of wood. But for its foundations, which were sheathed from the naked eye, it stood up from the ground a single story. Unlike the servants' building, though, it was replete with wide windows that smiled out onto the solitude around it.

Sweeping with his foot, Bet cleared away the gathered snow at the edge of the house's only door enough to afford a presentable entrance. Then he slipped a key in the lock, handed it to Sam and stepped aside for the lawman to enter.

The guest house was comprised of two rooms. The front boasted a fireplace and chairs gathered around it. Unlike the manor house, there were no decorations on the walls. No curious objects of antiquity to spur the imagination, only the gathered dust of neglect. It was simple and plain and, Sam judged, a more than adequate space for the next day or so. Until the storm blew past and he could return with William's body in tow.

"That all, Sheriff?" Bet asked, lingering by the door. "Everything fine?"

Sam nodded. "Yeah," he said. "Everything's fine."

As a final prodding, with good humor, Sam nudged the young man.

"Off with you now. Sleep the night."

"Yes, sir."

The door slammed shut behind him, the groaning wind suddenly silenced, and Sam watched Bet fight his way through the white across the grounds until he disappeared over the hill and beyond sight.

He turned around.

"Just you and me, love," he remarked to the empty space.

A copious store of firewood and tinder provided Sam what he needed to get a blaze going. He dragged a chair as close to the roaring flames as he dared and sat, thinking and reflecting. Considering the case at hand. He thought of the faces of the volunteers who had turned out for the search and wondered which one—or which *ones*—among them had known the boy's fate long before they showed up to tramp through the storm and then collect compensation from Charlotte Crownhill for their efforts. Or had it been some ghoulish desire to be close to the crime committed? He confessed to himself that he had not studied the men very well, for there was no assumption that something foul had occurred. He simply had not regarded them as suspects at the time.

It was yet another failing of his abilities as a lawman, and a mistake that his father would not have made. His father had known well the dark hearts of men and he had never regarded a soul as innocent until such was proven beyond doubt. Even then, to his mind, they were all guilty of some hidden black deeds, even if the light of the law did not come to shine upon them.

When the hour grew late, he retired to the dusty bed in the back of the guest house, sleeping in his clothes with his coat as a blanket. Miss Charlotte had made no steps to enhance his accommodations, though he would occupy them without complaint. She had been through much that day and seeing to his sleeping arrangements was likely a distant second to comforting her distraught daughter.

So fatigued was the sheriff, in fact, that after laying his head upon the pillow, he drifted right off to sleep, failing to even snuff the candle at his bedside.

Later, when he woke for a moment in the dim light of that fading candle, he made a vain attempt to crawl out of the dreams that enshrouded him like a grave. Before that could be accomplished, though, a familiar hand lighted on his shoulder and the sound of his father's voice filled the room as the man stood by his bedside. The moment was so familiar that Sam knew it must be a dream.

"Wake up and stand fast, boyo," his father uttered in his thick brogue. "They're comin' around the back way and ye'd better have more than yer knob in yer hand when they arrive."

"Da?" Sam groaned, bleary in the near darkness.

It had to be a dream for there was no other reason his father would be there, uttering those words again; words which echoed as small tortures in Sam's mind. Words that were a bitter reminder of how Sam had failed him one hot summer night long ago and how the old man had paid for it with his life.

Still, when he sat up in the guest house bed, he saw the old man's form lingering at the threshold of the small bedroom and he rose to follow him.

"Somethin' goin' on," his father said, turning the corner, "and ye'd better see to it."

As Sam put his first step forward on the achingly cold floor, he was suddenly aware that this was no dream. Something cold and wet mushed between his bare toes and he looked down to see what it was.

Snow.

Messy, irregular heaps of the stuff led away from his bed, out the door and around the corner. In the quiet of the guest house, he heard a rhythmic, wooden thumping.

He checked his side expecting to find an empty holster but felt the grip of his pistol there, drew it, and crept through the house to follow the path that his father had taken. His wits now about him, it wasn't that he thought his Da was actually present in the room. It was just that his dream of the dead man and the moment of his waking had intersected with something very real.

Someone had left these tracks of snow on the floor and it wasn't him.

Sam turned the corner from the bedroom and looked into the shadowed confines of the sitting room. He saw more lumps of snow staggered along the floor and the door to the guest house ajar, banging open and shut with the wind of the storm.

Then something else. The crunch of deep snow and a pressing against the house.

He froze, waiting, scanning the room.

As his gaze fell upon the wide window that looked out onto the wood, he saw a pale and deathly face looking in. The face of his father, returned to taunt his son.

He recoiled and brandished his pistol.

"But I have it this time, Da! See?"

Then the face was gone and something in its movement uprooted the sheriff from his frozen fear. Indeed, it had been a spectral face that he had glimpsed in the window, but it hadn't been his father's. And it had moved away quickly, not with the slip of a spirit but the clumsy gait of a man.

Sam ran to the door and kicked it open, looking out onto the white landscape of the grounds. Something wild was tramping through the snow in the direction of the manor house, pale and gangly looking, its thin white hair flying behind it.

"Stop there, you," he hollered out and gave chase, but before he could get very far, the figure disappeared into the shadows, incorporeal as the night itself.

The sheriff stood there, his heart pumping. On the far side of the main house, he saw an orange glow pulsating in the darkness. He barely sniffed the air before he smelled it; burning.

Something beyond the house was burning.

When he arrived at the servants' quarters, he found it consumed with flames that licked high into the winter night, uncaring of the snowstorm that still raged around them. He found that the servants had gathered a safe distance away from the conflagration, watching as the only home they had ever known burned to the ground.

They were a sorry lot; Colvin shrouding the wraithlike Seena from the punishing winds as Bet and Twig were doubled over, coughing smoke from their lungs.

"Y'all all right?" Sam asked as he ran up on them.

Colvin looked back at him with dark, tired eyes and nodded.

Looking around, Sam didn't see the young woman.

"Where's Mary?"

"She's in the big house, Sheriff."

Sam breathed a sigh of relief at this. When he heard the rustling of snow from behind them a moment later, he turned with his pistol drawn.

Three womanly figures lumbered toward them in the darkness, lanterns held aloft. Charlotte, Lucy and Mary. He lowered his gun arm.

"What has happened?" Charlotte called, her lilting voice scarcely able to pierce the driving wind.

"Done caught fire out yonder," Colvin said, glancing over them. "Y'all get on back inside now."

Sam surveyed the faces of the women and found them all staring at the inferno in abject, distant horror.

"Ladies," Sam began, asserting some authority, "he's right. What's done is done. Best go on back to the house now."

In the firelight, Charlotte's eyes smoldered at him for a moment before turning to Colvin's nephews.

"Boys," she commanded to Bet and Twig, "carry Miss Seena into the house. You all can stay in the downstairs rooms for the time being."

Colvin and Sam watched as the five of them limped toward the house, Bet carrying Seena in his arms like an infant and Twig helping the other women, their long nightgowns bogging down with snow and ice.

Once they were safely out of earshot, Sam turned to the big man.

"How did it start?"

Colvin shook his head.

"Ain't got no idea."

Sam sucked his teeth and nodded.

"It's a good thing you got the boy buried tonight, huh?" he remarked.

Colvin regarded him warily, then cast his eyes down the way he might have once regarded the field overseer.

"What?" Sam demanded. "What is it, man?"

The big man shook his head.

"Ain't never got the chance, Sheriff. Momma was sleepin' and I won't about to wake her with all that. Reckoned William won't goin' nowhere and the mornin' would be just as fine."

Sam Lock looked over at Colvin, his eyes narrowed.

Then he walked away without a word, back toward the guest house.

"What?" Colvin called after him. "You think I had a hand in this?"

The sheriff paused and turned, hollering his reply into the wind.

"No, but I think that whoever murdered young William set this fire. To cover his tracks and send me packing."

It was true that without a body and proof of the horrible wounds the boy had sustained, there was no case that he could bring for prosecution. But he wasn't about to let the Crownhills and their neighbors know that. He would see justice done, come hell or high water.

"But they don't know the law," he shouted. "And they don't know me."

He spat into the snow.

CHAPTER 4
DELVING

Impossibly, the weather the next morning had turned for the worse. Though the snow had slacked off some, the wind increased and it battered the house, howling as it rushed around the corners and among the eaves.

That afternoon, Sheriff Lock sat with Charlotte in the drawing room at the rear of the house, sipping hot tea. It might have seemed an idle moment to her but Sam was there to confront the lady of the house about a very specific matter.

"What happens now, Sheriff?"

"I'll be speaking with everyone today," he said. "There must be something that someone can offer, something they know, even if they don't realize they know it. There is no information unworthy of consideration, Charlotte."

Well, that had been awfully familiar of him. He turned and offered an apology.

"No," she replied. "It's fine if you call me Charlotte. You're a guest in my home, after all."

"You mean Mister Crownhill's home, don't you?"

She paused a moment.

"Yes, of course."

"Your father's away on business, is that right? Richmond."

She nodded.

"Bet seemed to think it was Williamsburg."

"He sometimes gets confused," she said, then quickly looked away.

"That right?" he said, leaning forward. "Ma'am, I'd like to know where your father really is and why he's not here looking after his family…and hasn't been here in some time from all I can tell."

She seemed to mull the question over.

"Is that a request or a demand, Sheriff?"

"Charlotte, I would prefer not to have to make demands."

Her shoulders dropped. "My father is not well," she said. "He hasn't been for years."

"So I've heard it whispered. Just how unwell is he?"

She rolled her eyes and sighed in exasperation.

"Very, Sheriff. He is *very unwell*. Hardly himself at all. He's being treated in a sanatorium outside of Richmond."

"Why didn't you tell me before?" he asked, though he could guess. Nothing so concerned the wealthy as scandal and the perception of weakness.

"As you said, he is a private man. Not to mention there is his reputation to preserve."

Sitting on the couch, she looked out the window and the white light of the day cast an ivory pallor over her skin. Sam thought that she looked for all the world like the statues of ancient Greece and Rome that he had read about, though there was something far more delicate about her.

"I thank you for your honesty," he said.

"And I for your candor, Sheriff."

"There's something else you should know about William's death," he said.

She cocked her head and furrowed her brow.

"There is—or was—evidence that leads me to believe it was not just an accident."

She stared at him, wordless, wide-eyed.

"But who…"

He shook his head.

"I can't say yet. Maybe I'll never know, but I'll find out what I can. It would be to satisfy my own curiosity, really, since there's little else I can do with the boy's body lost in the fire last night. Even if I had a suspect."

"Oh, dear." She sighed and closed her eyes even as tears came to their edges. "We'll never be able to bury him, will we?"

It was a terrible thing to realize and Sam could think of no words of comfort to offer. It occurred to him to mention that a search of the burned quarters may yield some bones they could put to rest but then that seemed rather too morbid a notion given her fragile demeanor.

Charlotte fretted silently in the conversation for a moment, and when she stood, her knee brushed the edge of one of the tea saucers and overturned the cup. She righted the cup with a shaking hand that was not steady enough to hold it and its wet handle slipped from her fingers and fell, breaking into pieces.

"Bet!" she called out. "Bring a rag. I've made a mess."

Then she was picking up the shards of the cup but her hands were no steadier and the sharp edge of one piece opened the tip of her finger.

She yelped and stuck the injured digit between her lips, sucking on it.

Sam went to her and took her hands in his own.

"I am so sorry, Charlotte."

They sat like that for a moment, their fingers entwined. Something passed between them that made both of them feel suddenly flush and warm and Sam's head swam from even this most innocent touch of her flesh.

Bet came hustling into the room, kitchen towels over his arm.

The spell was broken and they stood apart as the young man soaked up the spilled tea and wrapped the broken cup.

Sam had to wonder at what he was doing here. It felt like he was spinning his wheels, just spinning and slipping, gaining no ground. Still, with the storm outside, there was nowhere else to be. He may as well use his time wisely and gather whatever information he could.

"Will there be anything else, Sheriff?" Charlotte asked, at once rigid and formal again.

He straightened.

"Yes, actually. I'll need to speak with the young ones around here. I'd like to start with Lucy."

"Lucy? Is that necessary? She's a bit overwrought."

"I promise I won't keep her long."

With the cleanup done, Bet left the room. Sam watched Charlotte wringing her hands over his request. She was being a protective mother and he could hardly blame her for that. Especially given all the girl had just been through.

"Very well," she conceded. "Shall I fetch her now?"

"Yes, please." He took a seat as he watched her leave.

Lucy entered the room, her complexion as pale white as the storm that blew outside, dressed in a nightgown with a blanket pulled around her shoulders. Sam did not think the girl looked well and wondered if she was not coming down with something from the prolonged exposure to the cold.

He told her to make herself comfortable and added wood to the fire, taking a moment to stoke its flames.

"How are you feeling, Lucy?" he asked, returning to his seat.

The girl sniffled.

"Well enough, I suppose. I still feel a terrible chill sometimes, though."

She pulled her hair from behind her and draped it over one shoulder as she tightened the blanket. Sam noticed a necklace of brightly colored beads that hung around her neck.

"That's a lovely necklace," Sam said.

"Thank you. It was a gift from my grandfather."

"Wonderful," Sam remarked absently as he opened his notebook.

Through the crack in the door to the parlor, he could see Charlotte hovering nearby, pacing, ever the vigilant mother.

"Mary has one just like it," the girl said.

"From your grandfather?"

Sam watched as Lucy glanced to the crack in the door where her mother's eyes met her own for a moment.

"No, I made Mary's myself. Grandfather prefers there be distance between his family and his servants."

"But not you?"

Lucy shook her head and smiled.

"Not at all. Mary and I are like sisters," she said, then scrunched up her mouth. "Well, maybe more like cousins. The women in this family have to stick together."

He returned her smile.

"It sounds like you're all very close," Sam said, scribbling in his notebook. "Does that upset your grandfather?"

"Well, Sheriff, when the cat's away…"

Sam looked up from his notes mid-sentence to find the girl staring at him strangely. Her lips were parted and she bit gently down on that bottom bit of soft and supple flesh. Something inappropriate called to him. For a bachelor in his late thirties, his appearance was still that of a fair, younger man. He was not unaccustomed to women stealing glances at him and he supposed that, with Lucy being a girl of fourteen on the verge of womanhood, it was not unthinkable that she might see him in that light. It was brash but what adolescent was not given to brashness now and again? No, what made him most uncomfortable was how some part of him gloried in being seen that way.

He looked to the door but Charlotte was not there.

"…and the cat is away often," Lucy finished after a long, lingering moment.

Sam cleared his throat.

"Can you think of anyone who might have wanted to harm William? Or any reason why someone might have?"

She thought about it, her fingers fondling her necklace.

"I suppose it could have been anyone from the neighboring farms," she said. "There is no shortage of peasants around here."

He cocked an eyebrow.

"Peasants?"

"Yes." She sighed. "Small minds, pitchforks and torches. That kind of thing."

"Pitchforks?"

She stared at him a moment, then, exasperated, said, "They're simple folk, Sheriff. Afraid of anything and everything. The chest-beating simians."

Simians? He would need to look that one up. But still Sam waited, listening.

"If it ain't white, it ain't right. That's what they say around here."

She knows, he thought. *She knows William was a half-breed.*

"Interesting," he said and scratched a few lines in his book.

Lucy rose from her seat, the blanket slipping from her shoulders. She ambled over to the large window that looked out onto the rear of the property and stared out of it at the blinding white of the storm.

"Do you think it might have been one of them?" she asked. "One of the neighbors?" She reached out and touched the glass pane of the window and Sam imagined that he could feel the chill emanating from it.

"I can't say," he said.

"I don't know, either, Sheriff," Lucy said, her voice soft, a timid and trembling whisper. "What if...what if it's someone much, much closer?"

Sam stood and approached her, though her back was still to him.

"Now, why would you say that?"

She turned then and, breaking into tears, she thrust herself against him and laid her head on his chest. The suddenness of it was a shock to Sam and it made him very uncomfortable. Still, he slid his hands up her arms and gently patted her back.

Behind them, the door into the parlor creaked open. When he looked up, he saw Charlotte standing there, her hands by her sides and a wan look on her face.

"What's going on here?" she asked.

Sam quickly stepped away from Lucy.

"She became quite upset," he offered, though he could not meet her gaze.

Charlotte breezed past him and took her sobbing daughter into her arms.

"As I feared she might," she said, giving Sam a hard look. "Are you done with her, then, Sheriff?"

"Yes, ma'am."

Charlotte and Lucy swept out of the room and through the parlor. Bet stood there looking odd and helpless as they passed.

The exchange with Lucy had left Sam unsettled and out of sorts but there were more interviews to conduct. He took a deep breath and summoned the lawman back to the fore.

Sam's interview of Bet and Twig produced very little of value. They merely echoed what was already known about William. The boy was a guest of the Crownhills for the past few months while his parents were abroad and he had been a decent sort, friendly with all of the family, even the servants. When he inquired about the boy's ethnicity, they disavowed any knowledge, stating that the father was a dark-skinned, dark–haired man of European descent and that, as far as they knew, none of the folk in the area had had any particular problems with the boy.

When pressed, though, they did concede that if the boy had appeared anything other than white, the neighboring farmers might have taken issue with that. Asked to identify which farmers that would be, the boys stated that it would be all of them. The fact that Horace had freed his slaves was not something that sat well with many in the area, especially considering the conflict over the matter that was shaping up in the country beyond the borders of the Crownhill estate.

Seated in the drawing room, making notes, Sam dismissed the boys and asked that they send for the servant girl, Mary.

The two boys exchanged quick, sideways glances.

"Mary?" Bet finally spoke. "What for?"

Sam quit scribbling and looked up.

"You need not worry about that," he said, his voice gruff and tone curt. "Only that I need to speak with her."

"Yes, sir," Bet said. "I'll see if she's available."

Sam narrowed his eyes at the young man.

"Bet, speaking now as the sheriff of this town, see that *she is available*."

The young man nodded slowly and then left the room, his brother in tow.

Sam waited there for almost half an hour before the young girl came in and took a seat on the couch opposite him. Although understandably nervous, Sam tried to put her at ease.

"Your necklace is lovely," he offered, pointing to the circlet of beads. "Just like Lucy's."

"Yes, sir," she simply said.

Sam could tell she was afraid of him—afraid of what he might ask and what he might do. It was understandable. Seeing that there was no lightening the mood with her, Sam decided he would begin with the same line of questioning he had asked of Lucy and the others.

"Can you think of anyone who would wish William any harm?"

"No," she said, her head down, not meeting his eyes.

She seemed so profoundly different than when he had met her the previous night. So downtrodden. Sam let the moment linger, though, heavy as it was upon her.

"Mary," he said, "if there's something you know, I need you to tell me."

She fought back tears and she fought them well, steadying herself.

"William was a good boy, Sheriff. I can't think of no one who would hurt him."

Her words were resolute but her tearful eyes betrayed them.

"What is it, then, that's got you so upset?"

She stared at him, resentful.

"I ain't upset, Sheriff. I don't get to be. Like Grandma Seena says, it's up to us womenfolk to bear up and move on."

"Seena says that, does she?"

Mary nodded.

"You're older than Twig and Bet, aren't you?"

"Yes, sir. Grandma Seena reckons me to be twenty-five years."

"Your maturity shines through," he nodded, smiling. "So you knew Mister Crownhill before he freed your family. Before he became…ill?"

"Yes, sir. I did."

"Before you were freed, how did you find him? As a master, I mean. Was he kind?"

"Yes, very kind," she said, but the frown she wore said otherwise.

Mary was lying, though Sam believed that she did so not out of malice but obligation to the family and some secret kept between them. The girl was breaking, though, and a crack was forming in the wall of deception. Perhaps it was time for a different approach.

"So, Horace was kind to you?" he asked, his tone now gruff.

"Yes."

"Always kind back then? Even to a *slave girl* like you?"

She looked up at him with deeply wounded eyes. Tears streamed down her cheeks now and her lips trembled.

"Was he kind to William, too?" Sam demanded, nearly hollering at the girl, feeling her shatter with the utterance of every syllable. "Was he kind to William back then, too, Mary?"

"No!" she cried out, then retreated back down inside of herself, sobbing. "He hated him, Sheriff. Even when he was a baby, Master Horace hated William *so much*."

As sheriff, his father once took great pleasure in breaking a witness in such a way. He would have reveled in her sobs and offered nothing in return except to gloat, smug with his newfound knowledge. He would have held the knowledge over the girl's head like an executioner's blade, employing threats and further intimidation to gain more knowledge. Always more. Pushing her to the brink.

It was there inside of him, too; the inclination to do as he had seen his father do. But when he took over his father's position, he had made a conscious choice to be a different sort of lawman. Instead, Sam rose and went to the girl's side, draped an arm around her and gave a gentle and reassuring squeeze.

"Thank you, Mary," he whispered to her. "You've done well and you can go now. Would you like to go now?"

She sniffled and straightened. "Yes, I…I have things to do."

He nodded. "Of course you do."

Mary stood, wiping the tears from her cheeks and smoothing her dress, and then she was gone, leaving Sam alone in the drawing room with nothing at all but the thunderous impact of her words.

He leaned back on the couch, feeling momentarily satisfied even as more questions swirled into a storm in his mind. He rubbed his tired eyes. At long last, things were coming to light. The dead boy's parents were not indisposed, not traveling abroad.

Even when he was a baby, Master Horace hated William so much.

The boy had been a part of the family all along. Being a half-breed, the boy's existence would be a racial shame that might have drawn the ire of any number of the neighboring folk. It was not only possible that one or several of them regarded William with such contempt as to murder him; it was highly likely. After all, a Negro slave was considered property under the law and killing one—no matter the pedigree—was barely regarded a crime at all

It was a despicable standard, though, which Sam hated more than most.

But why the mutilation of the boy's genitals? That didn't seem the work of some yokel looking to teach the family a lesson about the boy's place in the world. Sam would have expected to find William shot or maybe even hanged. Unless it had been a message about halting the proliferation of such half-breeds, whose very existence was a clear offense to what many saw as the pure-blooded legacy of white men.

Even Sam's father would have viewed it as such and knowing that to be true was an embarrassment to his conscience. Though, as he considered it, he could not shake the notion that what was done to the boy was an act of impassioned hate perpetrated by someone who was gravely unhinged.

Lucy's haunting question came to him. *What if it's someone much, much closer?*

Indeed. Who would have borne the most shame for a half-breed living under the roof of Evermore—the bastard child of his only daughter, Charlotte, and one of his very own slaves? The sort of man who would have been incensed that the only male heir to his fortunes was a half-Negro boy. A man who was not in treatment hundreds of miles away but being kept hidden nearby, somewhere on the sprawling estate. What other reason would there be to keep the boy's true relationship to the family such a guarded secret, if not to protect the most likely suspect in the crime?

It was a farfetched notion, true, but Sam could not shake the feeling that once again, Miss Charlotte had been deliberately dishonest with him.

He glanced out the window and saw the chaotic winds sweeping across the land. Snow continued to fall but the flakes were smaller and less dense. The storm would soon be over.

Sam's mind focused on that idea, everything else becoming murky.

The storm will soon be over, he thought. *Soon it will be over.*

He repeated it in his head like a numbing mantra. A moment later, a sleepy, mournful air from distant memory reverberated in his mind and the sheriff closed his eyes.

"They're comin' around the back way and ye'd better have more than yer knob in yer hand when they arrive."

He breathed a question and when there came no reply, Sam was on his feet, navigating the labyrinth of the brothel's many chambers, bumping into walls as he endeavored to get his head about him. Too much whiskey from the night before still coursed through him, making him wobbly. Da had warned him against it, true, but what did the old man know?

A door that he thought led to the upstairs hallway opened into a closet that apparently served as privy of sorts, buzzing with flies and smelling of shit. At once, Sam put his arm across his face to block the odor and backed away, slamming the door on that putrid space.

He stumbled over entwined and sleeping bodies, their naked flesh slicked with sweat in the heat of the morning. The house was a good-time-shack up in the woods near a natural spring, where rowdy folk convened to gamble, fight and fornicate. A two story building that had once belonged to a farmer but was taken by the present owner to settle a debt between the two. In a turn of circumstance, that house now had the effect of luring others into debt at the behest of Adder Crane, who wanted to set himself up as Selburn's first and only kingpin of criminal enterprise. Crane's unfortunate misstep, however, was that in founding the Spring Creek house of ill-repute, he had not sought the partnership of the other men with similar, smaller interests in the town's illegal activities.

Sam had argued to let the degenerates have it and let the two gangs of vermin outlaws fight it out and they would arrest whoever was left standing. But there was no compromising with his father, an Irishman from the old country who had been trod upon by the English crown and couldn't wait to repay someone…anyone…in kind, whenever the opportunity presented itself. His father was the sort of sheriff that enforced the rule of law not by delegating from his office but by walking the trenches alone, mired deep in the mud and blood of rural anarchy. All his life, Sam had known it would one day be his father's undoing.

Sam came to rest behind a pile of firewood stacked on the back porch. His father, only feet away, leveled his flintlock rifle at the dark morning and commanded his son to be ready.

Sam nodded, his hand going to the holster at his side, and finding nothing.

"Shit," he blurted out.

"Left it inside, didn't ye?"

Sam nodded.

"Go and get yer steel, ye bleedin' fuckwit."

Those words, those words. The absolute last he would ever hear pass the old man's lips because as he crawled through the house, the triggermen of Selburn's rival gang were lighting the place up, shredding it with black powder flashes and a rain of piercing iron that felled every single person there, customer or not.

Except for him.

Except for Deputy Sam Lock, now hiding under the bed in the room where he had left his pistol. Cowering like a child. He dared not cry out or move. In the fog of fear and anguish, tears came to his eyes and his throat bobbed up and down, stifling the sobs that wanted to erupt. Sam lay there under the bed and wondered if they would find him as the gang of men walked the rooms of the brothel, putting down anyone who still drew breath—the sound of their boots in the quieting house like the grim tolling of a bell.

When he'd first got to the room, dashing about in search of his weapon, he had heard the moment of his father's defeat. The empty click of the rifle's hammer as the old man ran out of ammunition. The heavy, shuffling thud of the gang of men stepping onto the porch. The curses and barbed words they traded with him. The defiant sound of his father hocking up a wad of phlegm and spitting it in one of the men's faces.

Then two shots at close range.

After they shot his father in the belly, one of them knelt close to the old man and eviscerated him. Cut him open from balls to brains like he was fixing to dress a hog. It was an awful act for one man to commit against another.

That goddamned savage.

Sam bit his lip and listened to every last curse and scream, a maddening pillar of sound that snaked through the house to find and torment him. After far too long, it finally ended in the watery gurgle of his father's last breath. That sound like a baby's rattle as it passed his bloodied lips.

Sam jolted awake as he fell to the floor, then scrambled to his feet, retreating from the enemies of his memory. His panic sent him stumbling backward into a wall in the drawing room. He flailed, trying to right himself, and felt soft cloth give way at his touch.

As he got to his feet, his heart went into his stomach as he feared what he had done.

In the fog of dream, he had stumbled into some ornate tapestry. Manor homes of the wealthy were well known to display such artifacts, much like the armaments in the foyer. No doubt it was some family heirloom that was centuries old, and he had carelessly torn it in half.

Damn fool.

He cursed the nightmare and his own clumsiness, then stepped back for a better look at the damage. What he saw, though, confused him.

If it was a tapestry, it was the most unassuming he had ever seen. It had been meticulously crafted to match the wallpaper of the drawing room and its sides were not open and hanging loose but tightly tucked beneath a length of trim on either side. Nor had he torn the thing, for on both sides, the slit up the middle was neatly stitched from floor to ceiling where it disappeared into another bit of trim along the top.

It was not a tapestry at all, but a curtain.

Sam slipped his fingers in between the two lengths of heavy cloth and pulled them aside to reveal a dark opening. Air much colder than that inside the house rushed out.

It was an entrance to some other part of the house. One cleverly disguised to blend in with the drawing room's surroundings. Had he not happened upon it, he would have never known it was there.

"I'll be damned," he said.

In the light spilling in through the windows, he beheld a narrow stairway with a steep pitch that climbed above into some high, dark region of the Crownhill home.

The third floor, he realized—the one hinted at from the outside but concealed among the sloping rooflines, turrets and eaves.

During the search for William, Sam had spotted an overhang nestled unusually high up the wall at the rear of the house but Colvin had assured him it was a small attic space where they'd already looked for the boy. That rear balcony was the only exterior portal into the hidden floor.

There was also something else. A sound that lilted from above down to his ears, a high and pinched sound like the painful mewling of a cat.

Sam searched a moment and found a lantern near a bookcase in the drawing room. Striking a match, he set it to the wick and the lamp glowed with golden light as he held it before him, stepping up and into the darkness.

CHAPTER 5
ASCENSION

The bowels of the Crownhill house seemed to close in around the sheriff as he crept up the stairway and that high, weeping sound grew louder and louder with each step.

He had taken only a few of those steps when he paused and considered what he was doing. What if Charlotte or one of the others came looking for him only to find him disappeared from the drawing room where he was only minutes before? Legally speaking, he was within his rights as a peace officer to investigate wherever he chose but doing so might destroy the good will he had established among the family and servants.

Sam's father would have cared nothing about such things, going wherever and doing whatever he damn well pleased. But Sam was reluctant. After all, there was nothing to stop them from turning him out into the storm and back to Selburn where, surely, he would then never discover what had happened here.

The plaintive crying sound was ringing in his ears, though.

That was enough, he decided, to propel him onward, and damn anyone who couldn't understand that he must respond. After all, if it was a person, their life could be at stake.

He took the stairs slowly, careful not to make a sound. The lantern illuminated his surroundings but revealed nothing about where he was headed. For all he knew, the passageway stretched on into the darkness of forever.

But that was the fear talking, wasn't it? Nothing in this world was forever.

When he reached the top of the stairs, the crying sound faded away and as he held the lantern aloft, he saw that he had come up into the middle of the third floor, into what indeed appeared to be an attic. There was nothing *small* about it, however. It was a vast space, filled with old and decrepit things—some objects whose utility might be prolonged with some attention and repair, and others that had outlived their usefulness long ago. There were dusty crates of clothing and other personal wares, too, not all of it as old as Sam would have supposed.

But the sound had ceased and in its absence he felt suddenly exposed. If they were to find him now, what reason could he offer for trespassing into this area of the house?

The golden light flickered and cast dancing shadows about him.

A cat!

Yes, that would explain much. The family cat had ventured into the attic and, unable to find any means of egress, had become trapped.

With this idea, Sam felt the tension in his body subside. More than that, he was now keen on finding the wayward animal. Young girls often favored such pets and if he could find the poor thing and deliver it safely back downstairs, then he might be a hero to Lucy.

Sam smiled at this thought. It might even soften her typically adolescent and defensive response to him, this alien authority figure who had invaded her home. However, he noticed, the very moment the mewling had disappeared, it had given way to a larger sound. At first he thought it only the moaning of the wind outside but as he shuffled through the maze of disregarded things, this explanation satisfied him little. The wind was there, certainly, screaming high as it rounded the corners of Evermore, but what he heard now was a low hum. One so low, in fact, that he could feel it reverberating, ever so slightly, in his chest.

Or was that simply his heart? It was suddenly thumping, quick and loud.

He faltered and caught himself on a white painted bookcase. Rodents skittered across the floor and over the boxes. The lantern light was too meager to see more than what was directly before him and he leaned down for a look on the shelves. Like everything else, they were littered with gathered dust and the droppings of vermin, but there was one very curious item set apart from the others, in a dark corner of the middle shelf—an infant's tin rattle.

He plucked it from the shelf and held it closer to the light where he could see the detail embossed on the head of the rattle and as he moved it this way and that, the beads inside spilled over each other and produced that gentle, rushing sound that was so soothing to the young. Along the stem of its handle was an opening and after a moment of wondering, he recognized it for what it was.

Pressing his lips up to the opening, he gently blew across it and a shrill sound pierced the heavy darkness of the attic. The sound of the whistle was immediately followed by some movement far off out of the reach of the lantern's light.

Something, he thought, quite a bit larger than a rodent.

Sam stood still, placed the rattle back on the bookshelf and peered into the black.

"Who's there?" he called out, listening intently for some reply or further sign of motion.

Just as he was fixed to move, the mewling returned. Only closer this time, much closer. It was then that he recognized it; not the garbled drone of a perturbed cat at all.

It was, beyond any shadow of a doubt, the cry of an infant child.

But that was impossible, he reasoned. He had met the family and the servants, met them all. Lucy and William were the youngest and only Crownhill children.

Unless...

Sam began picking through the attic, listening for the sound to increase in volume.

He moved toward the sound but then it stopped.

After a moment, it started again, though this time it seemed to come from a different direction.

On and on it went, the crying starting up, reaching a crescendo and then abating into silence. Only to begin again.

After some time, and overwrought by his effort, Sam paused and listened.

The sound was coming not from any one direction but from all directions.

For a moment, he wondered if it was truly a sound at all, or if it was something else. A deep-seated anxiety, perhaps, given form but existing only in his mind.

All around him, the sounds. The buzzing in his bones, the crying in his ears.

Lost and confused in the yawning space of the attic, the incessant wailing assaulting him from everywhere and nowhere, his hand grasped something and it rocked to the side but did not fall. Holding the lantern to it, he saw it was a cradle.

He cleared a few objects that stood in his way, their disused remains clattering to the floor, until he stood next to a crib.

Sam craned his neck and peered into it.

A soft cotton blanket was still curled at the bottom of the crib…but there was something else.

Something was moving.

He gasped. There, amidst the rat droppings and the grime of years, was the pale hand and fattened cheek of an infant.

"My God," he breathed, reaching down to pull the blanket away as the child turned its head.

He drew back instantly at the sight of its ragged face, bits of its cheek blackened, a vacant socket where its left eye should have been.

Sam's fingers still held the blanket and as he teetered, the bit of moth-chewed cloth came with him and revealed the infant's body—a hideously deformed mass of tiny gears and spindles with a rusted key buried in its side.

Sam swallowed hard, catching his breath as his pounding heart calmed. The metal body, the exposed gears and the ceramic flesh of the head, arms and legs. It was a mechanized crawling doll, produced in the strikingly lifelike manner that the Germans were known for.

He shuddered and let go a sigh of relief that formed into a cloud of breath in the cold, black cavern of the attic.

It was a toy, nothing more.

But the cradle was real enough and as he shone the light around it, he saw other bits of furniture, other playthings and decorations that would have only been of importance to an infant. In the corner, there stood a squad of hand-carved wooden soldiers—British regulars in red coats, each man forever frozen, forever standing at attention with musket upright and with the stock tucked under the right arm. They looked as if they had barely been touched, though they were clearly the toys of a boy child.

"William," Sam whispered to himself.

The sheriff leaned over to replace the doll's blanket, snorted at himself, feeling foolish and embarrassed but still more than a little on edge. For the sake of certainty and his own comfort, he removed the key used to wind the doll and slipped it into the pocket of his trousers. As he did so and stood upright, chin up, a blade of light swept over the room from somewhere behind him, splitting the darkness briefly before a loud and wooden cracking sound sent his heart into his throat again.

When he turned to look, there was nothing. Sam held the lantern out and moved in the direction from where the light had come. As he stepped through the sea of objects that littered the attic, he saw an opening in the wall a few paces away and went to have a look.

There were stairs leading down, and a woody smell that eclipsed the mustiness of the attic. He knelt down and found bits of bark and threads of pulp—the droppings of firewood carried across the floor.

He stood and went back, examining the far wall for other seams or indications of a door of any kind. It was not long before he found it, just past a blind corner, amber light leaking out from around the edges.

Standing near the door, he could feel the heat emanating from the space. The room beyond was incredibly warm and it was kept so continuously if the amount of bark and tinder on the floor were any indication. There was something else, too. The low hum that he had heard throughout the third floor was loudest here.

Its source was just beyond the door.

Sam pushed against the door gently and found that it gave.

Should I knock? he wondered.

Hesitating in that moment, he heard his father's voice.

You're the bloody sheriff.

This time, he decided the voice was right.

He pushed against it a second time, much harder and the door swung open easily.

He stepped into the room beyond.

It was a small space and extremely unkempt. From what he could tell, there were no windows although a door in the rear wall opened onto the balcony he had seen on the rear of the house. To his left, an enormous fire blazed in a fireplace and it was only a moment before he was struck with the stifling heat of the room and began to sweat and itch beneath the collar of his shirt. It was a sensation that only worsened when his eyes fell on a man, wild and nearly tribal in his appearance, gnarled with age.

Horace Crownhill.

The man sat at a desk, not a stitch of clothing on, intently at work creating some object out of thin lengths of semi-rigid metal wire; the kind of material a jeweler might use.

He looked up from his work and stared absently at the sheriff, aware but uncaring that he had entered the room. Horace seemed in fair health, though it was clear that grooming and hygiene had ceased to be of great concern to him long ago. His color was healthy but when the man grinned at him, his smile was a broken crescent of yellowed, rotting teeth. His hair—what was left of it—was long and white and mussed, giving him an appropriately mad appearance that was dwarfed by the boundless lunacy that swam in the man's cold, blue eyes.

Horace returned to his work, plucking something from a glob of sweet smelling matter that sat nearby on his desk, then sliding it down onto a framework of metal that looked as if it had been molded into the shape of a crown. He plucked another and only then did Sam realize that the adornments were moving, squirming there along every inch of the wire crown. In between each shape, small, dark beads were strung on the wire. And there were more such creations littering the room, all of them filled with tiny, black shapes. Those same shapes lighted upon Horace's naked flesh like shifting warts.

Writhing and humming.

Then, again aware of the deafening buzz, Sam looked up and took a step back in horror. Along every foot of the joint where the walls met with the ceiling, nestled in every available crack and crevice were enormous honeycombed structures; paper thin and alive with the activity of thousands upon thousands of crawling, insectile bodies.

Wasps.

The old maniac was breeding them. Sustaining the vicious creatures even in the icy grip of winter with the roaring blaze in the fireplace. For what purpose only the insane could know, though it seemed in part for Horace to bejewel his creations with their crawling forms, flitting wings and undulating stingers.

Sam stumbled backward until he could feel the edge of the open door behind him and slid along it until he was stepping back into the darkness, the lantern dangling in his limp grasp. As he moved farther away in stunned silence and abject disgust, the sight of Horace Crownhill melted away and after a moment, Sam saw the young servant girl, Mary appear at the crack in the door.

She cast a sullen but apologetic glance at the sheriff and then pulled the door to, closing off the room and plunging him into the cold darkness of the attic once more, though he would not linger. Could not linger. He turned to scamper away toward the second staircase he had discovered but something was in his path, shambling toward him from the black.

The sound of grinding metal and ticking gears filled the space as it crawled into the light with its sweet face that had been rendered so grisly by neglect, ceramic arms reaching out as chubby, cream-colored knees driven by the gears propelled it forward.

He recognized that it was only the crawling doll, though he could not understand how it had gotten here when he had left it in the cradle. He shoved his hand into his pants pocket and found the doll's key there. Exactly where he had put it. His mind bent and the world reeled around him. What was it doing there in the middle of the floor and how...how in God's name had the ghastly thing been *wound* into motion?

The sheriff cried out, a breaking whimper that belonged not to a man but a frightened boy, then he lurched forward, taking wide strides over and around the creeping doll. As he took the first step down the narrow stairway, he could not help but cast an eye back the way he had come. Perhaps it was morbid curiosity. Perhaps it was primal fear. From the corner of his stolen glance, he saw the baby as it continued across the floor toward the golden light seeping out from under the door to Horace Crownhill's throne room, where the King of Wasps reigned with deranged abandon.

Sam ran, his footsteps thundering down the steps. The second staircase seemed even narrower than the first. As he went, the darkness and the innards of Evermore squeezed him through, ejecting him like an unwanted thing.

He was happy to comply.

The flimsy door at the bottom opened into a pantry with shelves full of goods. Bags of flour, sugar, sacks of dried herbs and rows of salted ham. Beyond the tiny space, another door beckoned. He burst through it into the warmth of the kitchen where the old woman, Seena stood with an absurdly large knife in her grasp, carving a roasted hunk of beef.

The aroma of cooked meat and spices was thick in the air and as he stumbled forth, she regarded him with great surprise. Disheveled and desperate to escape the house, he couldn't even manage the words to excuse himself as he went out the back door and trotted across the grounds and through the snow to the guest house.

Once inside, he bolted the door and fell into a chair in the sitting room. The house was cold and his ragged breath escaped his lungs in puffs of steam. The world spun around him and his guts felt sour. He reached for a nearby chamber pot and dry heaved over it.

Sam struggled to understand what he had seen in the attic of the manor house. He reasoned that the crawling doll must have been a strange trick played upon him by his own mind. He had spent too much time out in the elements and, as a result, he was falling ill. Perhaps there was some fever upon him. Fevers were well known for causing delirium. That must be it.

It explained the frightful vision of the doll well enough but the heat of Horace Crownhill's chamber of horror had been real and both the man's presence at the estate and his insanity were now undeniable. In such a state, the old bastard was capable of any number of demented things and the murder and mutilation of the boy, William, was certainly among them.

Sam gathered himself enough to kneel at the hearth and start a fire. After a few minutes, he had the logs roaring as smoke billowed upward into the chimney. The guest house was growing dark as the sun began to set behind the clouds loitering in the sky.

He heard a knock at the door.

"Yes?" he called out, unable to move himself from the hearth and the growing warmth of the flames.

"Sheriff, you all right? There's supper in the house."

It was Bet lingering at the threshold.

"No!" he shouted.

Then, realizing how uncontrolled that had sounded, he offered an explanation.

"No, thank you," he softened. "Please give Miss Charlotte my regards. I…I'm not feeling well, I'm afraid."

"All right, then," Bet said.

Sam lay there on the hearth, listening to the boy crunch away back to the manor house through the snow. When he was gone, the sheriff closed his eyes. He tried to forget the macabre things he had seen in the attic of the manor house. He tried to forget the lurid sight of the doll turning its head as he pulled the blanket back. Most of all, he tried to ignore the sound that had followed him out to the guest house and even now persisted.

The tortured cry of an infant child, as clear as a bell, rang in his ears, though again he doubted his senses.

It was a fever. It must be.

It must be.

CHAPTER 6
THINGS UNSAID, THINGS UNSEEN

A pounding stirred him awake and he rose in anger, ready to let loose upon the servant boy. He had made his refusal of supper quite clear, had he not? And still the lad was hanging about, rapping on the door. As he went to it, he noticed the room was dark now as was the sky, and only a modest orange glow from the quickly dying fire lit the room at all.

When he threw the door open, Charlotte Crownhill was the last person he expected to see.

Still, there she was, standing against the backdrop of falling snow, a basket cradled in her arms.

"Do you mind if I come in?"

It was most unusual for the lady of the house to pay such a visit to a gentleman guest, especially after nightfall. But then these were accommodations she had provided, so who was he to refuse?

He stepped aside and swept his arm to welcome her in, then shut the door behind her.

"Your fire's cold," she observed, setting down the basket and kneeling to stoke the flames.

"I nodded off, it seems," he offered, and then went to her. "Please, you don't have to do that."

"Nonsense," she declared. "Bet tells me you aren't feeling well. A warm fire will do you good."

He thought of Horace and the inferno of his room and of…but he pushed away further thoughts.

"I'm feeling much better," he said. "I suppose I must have been fatigued. Some rest seems to have done wonders."

"Wonders?" she asked over her shoulder, looking him up and down, her expression dubious.

He managed a sheepish smile.

"Well, perhaps not *wonders*."

She tossed another few logs onto the embers and coaxed the flames to life, then stood to face him.

"I brought some of the roast for you and bread," she said as she pulled the items from the basket.

Among them was the decanter of whiskey and two glasses.

In the brighter light, Sam noticed the glaze over her eyes and realized that she had been drinking.

"Miss Crownhill—"

"Oh, let's not resurrect all the formalities again, Sam," she said as she poured a glass and handed it to him.

It was not proper for a man and a woman, so casually acquainted, to be taking drink together but then if she had been drinking and her inhibitions were broken down, she might finally provide the answers that he needed to confirm his suspicions about the family's history and the boy's death.

He sat and took a sip from the glass, watching the fire crackle and hiss.

Charlotte remained standing, her back to him, her eyes lost in the flames as well.

"Charlotte, I have quite a few questions about what has gone on around here. And I reckon it's time you gave me some *honest answers*."

"I was afraid you might say that."

He watched her, standing there backlit by the flames, her shape as eloquent and inviting as the rolling hills of the Blue Ridge in springtime. So enchanted was he that, for a moment, he completely lost his thoughts.

"What can I tell you, Sam?" she asked, turning and breaking him from his trance.

What was it he wanted to ask? He took another sip of whiskey.

"I found *the third floor* today, Charlotte."

A chip formed in her perfect, debutante facade and then crashed to the floor.

She sank the whiskey in her glass and sat down across from him, her eyes twinkling in the firelight as tears came to them. If they were manufactured as a ploy to soften his approach, she would find them in vain.

"Your father is well beyond ill, ma'am," he stated flatly. "I would say that he is quite possibly the most demented person I have ever laid eyes on."

She stifled a sob and nodded.

"I can understand why it was you wanted to keep him from me," he offered. "However, I believe he is given to run amok."

"Father hasn't left the third floor in months."

Sam snorted, thinking of the phantom that had tracked snow into the bedroom of the guest house, knowing now that it had been no phantom at all but the lunatic old man. No doubt still in possession of all the house keys, he had let himself inside to stand at the sheriff's bedside watching him sleep.

The notion chilled and repulsed him.

"You're wrong on that account, Charlotte. Why, he paid me a visit just last night."

She regarded him with surprise.

"I didn't know it was him, of course. Not until today."

"Who did you suppose it was before today?"

Sam shrugged and shifted in his seat, thinking of the vision of his father's ghost.

"I suppose I just thought it was some lunatic..."

He drifted off then, his eyes downcast. After all, it had been some lunatic. Charlotte went again to the decanter and freshened up their glasses.

"There is something else I need to ask you about, Charlotte."

"Yes?"

"While I was in the attic, I saw—"

Terrible, terrible things. Things that cannot be.

"I came upon a cradle and some things that once belonged to a child. They were William's things, weren't they?"

She stood and, swirling her glass in both hands, turned away from him to look into the fire.

"What?" she replied. "Why would William's baby things be there in the house?"

Sam sighed, weary of this game of denial.

"Because William was no guest. He was always here. I know that now."

Silence.

"No point in denying it or making something else up," he said. "The girl, Mary, told me how little your father always cared for the boy. Considering his…mixed origins…I suppose it's understandable why."

She turned on him, the corners of her mouth trembling in anger.

"Is it? Why should a man feel such disdain for a child? I don't think there's anything understandable about that at all, Sheriff."

He was surprised by her anger and it took him a moment to recover.

"I didn't mean it quite that way."

Her eyes softened then, flitting about the room as she took a sip from her glass. He did likewise and for a moment they were there before the fire, drinking in silence. Sam could not judge how Charlotte felt at that moment, for she appeared to be quite capable of holding her liquor, but his head was light and buzzing with the whiskey, his inclinations teetering toward the indulgent.

Lord God, she was a beautiful woman! Even with the troubled expressions she now wore on her face as he unraveled her lies before her, she was nothing less than exquisite.

"So those *are* your son William's things in the attic, then?"

She glanced up at him, her expression slack and suddenly confused.

"What? No, they aren't William's," she said, gazing into the flames once again. "My father insisted that William be raised in the servants' quarters, of course. He would have never been afforded such fine things, having been born a slave."

"A slave?" Sam said, confounded. "But he was—"

"William is not my son, Sheriff. He's Mary's," she said, adding, "or he was."

Sam sat there a moment, sipping his drink. It made sense, of course, as he recalled how grief-stricken Mary seemed when he spoke with her.

"But he was of mixed blood," he said, trying to work it out.

Charlotte gave a bitter snort and drank.

"Father took a shine to Mary very early on, you see. Many nights, he summoned her from her quarters into his own. There, he took her. Night after night."

The dark implications of her words settled upon him.

He *took* her.

It was a heinous act in Sam's estimation, but unfortunately the phenomenon of masters forcing themselves upon their female slaves was both common and accepted. Children of such a union were common as well, though they were always kept a dark family secret if they were kept at all. Most were sold off to another plantation. Or worse.

"Eventually, she came to stay with him all the time. Right here in this very guest house. It's why Father had it built."

"A forced relationship, no doubt."

"At first." Charlotte sighed. "But by the time she was with child, they were out here together. It was so strange, the way he was—sweet with her, really. He seemed so pleased when she was carrying the boy but the night of his birth, when the child was pulled from her, screaming and crying, he changed instantly. He saw nothing of himself in William. He looked upon him with such contempt, I shall never forget it."

Tears rolled down her cheeks.

"But I believe that children yield what you invest in them," she continued. "Like any crop, you must sow and tend the field with care. Do that and the harvest will be plentiful. Imagine what William might have been if my father had taken the time to love and care for him."

"Yes, well, as you said, there is your father's reputation to consider."

"Fair enough," she said, wiping away tears.

"Did you know, Sheriff, that when a child is born, you can hardly tell his race at all? They all come out red and pinched, the little ones. White or Negro or Indian or otherwise, they all look the same at first."

She finished her drink and turned to him.

"Sort of plumbs at a deeper truth, don't you think?"

He nodded but he didn't know. His head was swimming, this knowledge commingling with the liquor as Charlotte was waxing philosophical. Such abstract things were not exactly Sam's strong suit. Instead, his thoughts turned to William's age, and the age of young Mary.

"It was William's fourteenth birthday that night, wasn't it?" he whispered. "At twenty-five years now, Mary would have been—"

"Eleven," Charlotte finished his thought darkly. "She was eleven years of age."

Sam shook his head. That was too young, just too young. A thing made all the worse by Horace having forced himself on her.

"My father was…is…a cruel animal, Sheriff."

And a murderer, Sam thought but did not speak it.

He blinked then, coming out of the fog of his thoughts. In that moment, he saw Charlotte Crownhill for the supple, tragic beauty that she was. Like a starling with a malformed wing, being a Crownhill had been both boon and bane to her.

Before he quite realized it, Sam was before her, his arms reaching for hers, his lips inches from hers.

Then they joined together in a moment of rough passion. They set their glasses on the table next to the decanter, their hands exploring each other's bodies, unclasping, unbuttoning as they kissed hungrily.

Charlotte and Sam stumbled down the hall to the bedroom not as two but as one—and when they fell into the old feather bed and he pushed up into her, she crossed her legs around him with welcome.

They made desperate love to one another there in the darkness of the dusty old bedroom and when they slept afterward, it was the rapt and heady sleep that only lovers and angels know.

Sam opened his crusted eyes and nestled into the soft curls of Charlotte's hair. He took the humming sound in his ears for the remnant of a dream, a dark thing that he cared not to dwell on. After all, there was a beautiful woman lying next to him, her porcelain curves hidden under musty sheets, her bare flesh against his own.

But he could not find sleep again—not in the bone-chilling air of the room. It wouldn't do to have a lady like her wake to such poor conditions, so he rose from the bed, pulled his trousers on and went into the sitting room to revive the dying fire.

After some effort, he got a good blaze going and warmth soon emanated from the hearth, filling the small space and radiating down the hall to the bedroom. He sat in a chair and eyed the nearly empty decanter of whiskey, rubbing his temples to soothe the dull ache that was growing somewhere between them.

The pale light of early dawn was gradually filling the maudlin sky and the world outside seemed cast in shades of blue and white. Leaning his head back, basking in the warmth of the flames, Sam thought of all that he learned the night before. He had always envied folk like the Crownhills; well-heeled families of high birth with lavish comforts and the wider world so within their reach. But if bearing the weight of such dark secrets was the price of a privileged life, then let them have it. He would take his own lowborn, stringent and cantankerous father over being a Crownhill any day.

His eyes felt heavy and as he closed them, the humming sound came once again. If it was to a dream he must go, then he would not fight it. But after a moment, he was still there awake. And the humming persisted.

Sitting up, he looked around the room and out of the corner of his eye, outside of the window, there was a movement—a shadow passing by. Sam was on his feet then, stepping into his boots. His gun belt was draped over the back of a chair and he pulled the pistol from its holster as he crept toward the door. He imagined Horace Crownhill, nude and barking mad, skulking around the guest house wearing a wire crown adorned with hundreds of buzzing, dying wasps. Secretly, he hoped for the old man to give him cause to shoot, for there was now no doubt in his mind about who had brought young William to his horrible end.

As God as his witness, and even with the man's daughter bedded and sleeping only feet away, Sam would put Horace down for good if given a reason.

Cocking the hammer back, he eased the door open and stepped out into the snow.

He peered around the guest house, into the stands of nearby trees, but saw nothing. Looking down into the snow, he could not tell for certain if someone had been standing by the door because whatever tracks might have been made were disappeared amidst those belonging to him and to Charlotte. And there seemed to be no tracks leading away from the door but those to and from the manor house.

Sam would have found this comforting except for the humming that he still heard. It sounded even louder outside. He moved to the right of the door and peered around the corner of the cabin—nothing, then to the left of the door, nothing there either.

Sam lowered his pistol and shrugged, dismissing it as nerves and whatever it was that had rattled his mind. Then he heard snow crunch from somewhere behind the guest house.

Carefully, he slinked along the side of the house and brought his pistol up at the ready.

Again came the crunching sound of snow and he stopped, listening.

Once, twice, three times, each with a brief pause in between—like the footsteps of a man.

He surged forward to the back corner of the house and when he rounded it, he saw someone standing twenty paces away.

"You there," he called out. "Hold."

The figure's back was to him and if it had been moving before it stopped now.

In the dim light, he struggled to see details. Was it Horace? He didn't think so.

"Identify yourself," he commanded but there came no reply.

As he looked closer, he could see the figure dressed in a shirt and ragged coat and dark trousers that clung so tightly to the legs it was as if they weren't there at all.

"All right," he said. "Turn around. Do it slowly."

Sam glanced down at the snow to see the figure's tracks leading away from the house but there were none. When he looked back up, it was turning toward him.

Its caramel skin had whitened and its eyes were empty and opaque. A shock of dark, curly hair sat atop its head. It wore no pants after all, its lean legs bare where they disappeared into the snow.

And the red. Oh, God Almighty, the red.

The crimson mess where its crotch should have been, the wider stain that covered the white shirt beneath the coat. The cold skin and empty eyes.

"William?" Sam said.

But it couldn't be.

The boy opened his mouth to speak and Sam waited to hear the words but as William's lips parted, a teeming horde of sleek wasps—striped brown and black and yellow—poured forth, crawling up the boy's face, over his eyes, and down his torso in an endless stream of humming wings and tiny, clacking legs.

Sam stumbled backward.

"No," he whimpered, shaking his head.

It came toward him now, though it made no disturbance in the snow about its legs.

"No, no, no," he insisted, shutting his eyes against the sight.

When he opened them, William was still there, still drifting toward him, a horrendous figure alive with crawling pestilence.

The sheriff's fear broke and gave way to anger. He brought the pistol up and aimed.

"No!" he shouted at the thing. "You're not here."

He pulled the trigger and the gun blasted forth, the recoil tipping it backward in his grip.

Then the hammer was cocked again and the trigger pulled as another blast pierced the cold morning and went zipping through William to land with an eruption of white somewhere far behind him.

"You are...not...here," he cried out as he marched toward it.

The trigger pulling now, again and again, and Sam unable to stop himself.

"You're...not...here, goddamn you!"

Click, click.

The gun was empty, the chamber spent, but still he pulled the trigger over and over.

Click, click, click.

"Sam?" he heard a shrill cry from behind him and turned, the pistol still up.

Dressed in her unlaced boots and with nothing more than a blanket wrapped around her, Charlotte, seeing the gun leveled at her, winced and moved aside. When Sam realized it was her, he dropped it to his side.

"What in God's name are you *doing*?" she screamed at him.

He hesitated a moment, his other arm shooting out to point behind him.

"Don't you see? He's..." the sheriff began, though as he turned to look again, he saw there was nothing. Nothing at all but a field of snow now pockmarked with bullet holes.

"There was..." he struggled to explain.

She was next to him now.

"What? What was it?" she asked. "Was it Father?"

Looking at her, he saw grave concern and terror in her eyes.

"No," he said, still glancing over his shoulder. "It was...I thought I saw something."

She glanced behind him and shook her head.

"Well, there's nothing there now, Sam. Come. Come back inside."

She laid a hand on his bare arm and gripped it, pulling him back toward the front of the house.

"I thought..." he stammered, bewildered.

Am I going mad? he wondered.

She pulled him through the door and back inside and they both collapsed in front of the hearth and the roaring fire he had made just moments ago.

She covered him with a blanket and held him tight as he shivered, blinking his eyes over and over to shake the vision of the dead boy from his thoughts.

CHAPTER 7
A MORBID ORNAMENT

It was not long after Sam had finally calmed down that the door of the guest house flew open and Bet came rushing inside. He searched about the place and when his eyes fell on the two of them huddled in front of the fireplace, he breathed a sigh.

"Miss Charlotte, are y'all all right?"

She covered herself with the blanket and nodded.

"Yes. Yes, we're fine."

The young man looked from her to the sheriff.

"He sure don't look fine."

She placed a comforting hand on Sam's shoulder.

"We had a bit of a scare," she said. "But he's all right now, aren't you, Sheriff?"

Sam looked up at the boy.

"I'm fine," he managed.

The young man lingered there in the doorway, though, looking no more relieved than when he had burst in on them.

"Bet?" Charlotte asked, becoming concerned. "Bet, what is it?"

The boy hesitated.

"There's...something. Up at the house. Y'all best come see."

She nodded her understanding.

"Just give us a moment to dress."

"Yes, ma'am," he said and stepped outside, waiting for them.

They dressed quickly and as Charlotte laced up her boots, Sam plugged fresh rounds into the chamber of his pistol and then holstered it at his side. She eyed the weapon warily.

"You sure you're all right?" she asked.

"I'm fine," he said.

"What did you see out there, Sam?"

Part of him—the small part that didn't suppose he was going mad—wanted to tell her. To tell her of the things that he had seen, all of them, in one long exhalation. He had the sense that she would not judge him and, after all, it would do some good to share these things that his mind was burdened with. It was such a weight to bear. But after what happened with his father, Sam Lock had become practiced at bearing awful things in silence.

"It was nothing."

She regarded him with a piercing stare.

"I don't believe you," she said.

He sighed.

"Another time, then."

"Very well."

She reached her hand up for him to help her off the floor.

They joined Bet outside and the three of them went trudging through the snow toward the manor house that lay beyond the woods at the top of the hill. The snow had stopped and there was now only the cold wind of a winter day. The sun was risen now, but still hidden behind thick, gray clouds.

The troubled expression that Bet wore never faded and he took his steps through the white-covered land wordlessly. No matter how often Charlotte attempted to pry information from him, the boy only shook his head, and muttered, "Best y'all see for yourselves, ma'am."

But before they saw anything, they heard.

A low and mournful groan that came not from the wind, for it had diminished to little more than a stiff breeze. It was the sound of a man's voice, and both Charlotte and Sam recognized the timbre of it to be Colvin's. However uneasy they had been before, their dread was doubled upon hearing the big man's voice in distress and Charlotte quickened her pace to such a degree that it was all Sam and Bet could do to keep up with her.

Cresting the hill that brought them to the back of the house, a low moan escaped Charlotte and before Sam could reach to grab her, the woman was barreling toward the house as fast as she could manage against the drifts of knee-high snow.

The crescent-shaped patio at the back of the house had been routinely cleared during the storm by Bet and Twig, making the final accumulation there little more than a few inches. Sam looked and saw Seena there, bent low next to Colvin, who was kneeling in the snow with his hands clasped at his waist, weeping and staring up as if looking into the terrible face of God Himself. Paces from both of them, Twig milled about with his hands shoved into his pockets and his head down.

Sam followed Colvin's gaze and beheld the young woman, Mary, floating high above them all.

Floating? How can that be?

Looking again, he saw that she was not floating but had been hung. Her neck was bent unnaturally and her head and the drape of her dark hair lolled as her body swayed like the pendulum of a clock in the chill and steady breeze, a morbid ornament festooning the cold and callous house of the Crownhills.

Crimson rivulets, now frozen, cascaded down her nightgown from the nearly invisible noose that encircled her neck. As Sam stepped onto the patio, he could see for certain what he suspected only a few feet before. The poor girl swung not from a length of rope but a strip of steel wire as long as she was tall. The kind of steel wire that Horace, the Mad Wasp King, used to construct his abhorrent creations. The other end of it was knotted tightly around the stone railing of the balcony just off of the old man's third floor chamber of horrors.

In the snow below her feet lay her wire necklace, now broken, the colorful beads scattered on the hard-packed snow.

Colvin's anguished moans were joined then by the terrible sobs of Charlotte Crownhill, who stumbled to her knees with her head and its locks of sun-golden hair held in her hands.

"Mary done this," Colvin blubbered, the strong features of the big man seeming to melt away with his rolling tears. "Oh, Lord, why has she done this?"

Sam felt moisture come to his own eyes but he wiped it away and stood there, feeling impotent to help any of these suffering folk. The girl certainly had more reason than most to take her own life. Her child had been defamed, hated and then murdered by the man who had been master and lover and father. Perhaps she had known all along that it was Horace who killed the boy out by the old barn. After all, she was the only one to spend any significant amount of time with him, looking after him day in and day out. And how horrible that must have been over the past few days, caring for the man who had murdered their son.

Sam's mind kept returning to the image of her closing that door to Horace's room on the third floor, the resigned look of sorrow on her face. God rest her soul, but even the most stone-hearted of folk could hardly blame her for taking such a desperate way out of her misery.

Except Sam Lock wasn't buying any of it.

As he looked above, he saw Horace milling about in his room. Then, almost as if on cue, the old lunatic emerged onto the balcony, extending his arms outward and bending his head as he closed his eyes, a profane mockery of the crucified Jesus, the crown of thorns replaced with one of bare wire and crawling, devilish insects.

"Mary didn't do this," Sam spat at the others. "It was done *to her*."

Did they not see what he saw? How could they be so blind?

Colvin's weeping ceased then, turning to silence at the sheriff's words. The big man followed Sam's eyes up to the balcony and, all at once, Sam could see that he understood. Colvin got to his feet, his praying hands now clenched into fists.

"Bet, Twig," Sam called out.

The young men approached him, both looking ashen and heavy of heart.

"Sir?" Bet replied.

"Cut the poor girl down. Wrap her up but keep her intact. I may need to return for the remains."

"Yes, sir," they replied in unison.

"Then," he continued, "if you can manage a lock, use it. If not, use whatever you can find in the attic—furniture, crates—and block the exit from Mister Crownhill's room. Hell, nail the damned door shut for all I care," he commanded, pointing to Horace on the balcony. "But *that thing* does not leave this house until I say so, understand?"

They nodded, though the sheriff did not wait to see it. He stormed across the patio.

"I can help the boys with that," Colvin offered.

The sheriff paused a moment to regard the big man with a look of deepest sympathy. But Sam knew that if he wanted to keep Horace alive, he had better keep Colvin away from him.

"Probably best if you stay with me until I leave here," he said.

Behind him, Charlotte called out.

"Where are you going, Sam?"

He turned and fixed her with as much compassion as he could manage for a man whose blood was boiling hotter with the passing of every second.

"I'm going back to Selburn this morning," he replied. "And I'm taking your murdering cur of a father with me. In shackles."

She made no protest and it was just as well, for he would not be dissuaded, not even by matters of the heart.

As Sam stepped off the patio into the snow, with Colvin following close behind, he saw young Lucy inside, standing at the window in the drawing room. She had been a silent witness to the whole ugly affair and as her gaze drifted skyward, he knew that she could see nothing more than Mary's lifeless, dangling feet.

Thank God for small mercies, he thought.

But then, trapped as Lucy was within this family, there was little comfort to be found. The venom of the things she had witnessed long before this tragedy had to have taken a toll on her, despite how well her loving mother had shielded her from them. As he passed by, her ice blue eyes fixed on him but seemed to look far beyond. In the midst of this new family horror, her face was dull with indifference as something in her mind disconnected itself. His heart went out to her, knowing that more than all of them, she would be haunted by these tragedies the longest.

Sam ached to offer words of comfort to the girl but now was not the time. As he and Colvin trekked through the snow toward the stable where Cutter waited, he was given to wonder if the young girl would ever take comfort in anything ever again.

CHAPTER 8
EGRESS

Sam pulled the girth under Cutter's belly, strapped and buckled it. In the shelter of the stable, with inches of straw at their feet, it was warm even without a fire. Colvin stood by near the stall of a chestnut pony with a white stripe down the center of its face.

He cinched the final buckle and slapped the hard leather saddle, wiping the sweat from his brow.

"It's so cozy in here, we all ought to sleep on beds of straw, don't you think?"

He watched as Colvin gave the animal a final stroke and sauntered toward him.

"Old slave trick," Colvin said.

"What's that?"

"Used to take the old horse blankets...they switch them out every year, you know...squirrel away some of the straw here and there. Then Momma'd sew it all up together. White folks'll put that pan of hot coals underneath their feather bed but I'd take straw over it any day. Surely would."

Sam chuckled, nodding his head.

"That's pretty damn smart."

The big man stood still, no real expression on his face apart from a nod and grin of acceptance that was so practiced from years of servitude.

"A freed man like you, along with your nephews," Sam continued, "only need go as far as Richmond. Take up a trade and have a life all your own."

Colvin fixed him with a sour, doubtful expression.

"Well," Sam qualified, "mostly your own anyway. At least there won't be an overseer or master to answer to anymore."

Colvin snorted a laugh.

"Sheriff, we all got a master to serve. Freeborn as you are, even you got a master."

Sam reflected on the truth of that. Even the sheriff's betters had betters that they answered to, and on and on it went, up the chain until it ended at God Himself.

"Colvin," Sam said a bit more plainly, "I think you ought to leave. Take the boys and Seena and clear out of here. After Horace is charged in court... even if he's not convicted...when the details come out, when they see how headsick he is...it'll never be the same around here."

"How do you mean?"

"Horace has business associates," Sam explained. "I expect that since his illness, he's been a silent partner and his lawyer has handled most of the decisions but it's the Crownhill reputation that binds them together. When they hear about him or see the way he is...the things I intend to accuse him of in court...the things they'll say about him in the newspapers...he'll be ruined. Forever."

"What about Miss Charlotte and Lucy?"

Sam sighed.

"I hope to convince her to move on as well," he said and then glanced out the stable door at the vast estate of Evermore and shook his head. "There'll never be peace of mind, not here. Not for anyone. God help me for sounding like my old man but I'm starting to think that, somehow, it's *this place*."

The two men shared a dark look of agreement.

"You seen things, ain't you, Sheriff?"

Sam couldn't bring himself to respond but Colvin nodded at the weary look in his eyes.

"I seen 'em, too," he whispered. "There's evil here, Sheriff. Like a river underground that poisons everythin'. You know it now, well as I do."

Sam couldn't help but agree. He had come to Evermore as a man of reason but he would leave it now, thinking it cursed, and praying that its black nature did not follow him. As they led the mount from the stable, hooves and boots crunching in the fallen snow, Sam looked over at Colvin.

"You want to kill him, I know."

Colvin pursed his lips. The big man could hardly deny it. There was no point in trying.

"Trust me when I tell you," Sam said further, "that you don't want that burden. You'll drag it around the rest of your life like chains."

"Yes, sir," Colvin said, though it was only out of habit. "Done a lot of bad things in my day, too."

Sam thought of those men who had cut his father down while he hid under the bed. After the smoke had cleared at the brothel, he had sought them out and rained vengeance down upon them one by one until they were no more. He remembered the last one best of all—one of the triggermen, a young thug named Paul Gentry who may have had a different life had he not fallen on hard times and in with the wrong people. It was suppertime when he came for Paul, and Sam remembered well the horror on the faces of the man's wife and children as he ushered them into the bedroom at gunpoint so they wouldn't have to see. But Sam could see it all, even now. Paul, seated at the supper table with his head bowed in a final prayer—this villain who had shot up the whorehouse without discrimination and done who knows what else—daring to petition God.

Sam put the barrel of the shotgun to the back of Paul's head and blew his brains out the front, all over the table and into the steaming bowl of stew set before him. In the years since, Sam had lost count of how many times, when in the thrall of some nightmare, he had eaten from that bowl with bits of gray matter and bone floating in it.

The sheriff clapped the big man on his shoulder.

"Believe me, Colvin," he said. "You ain't so bad."

The two of them led the horse down the white hill and toward the manor house in silence.

Before leaving, he climbed up to the third floor again to sweep Horace's room for additional evidence but Sam found nothing. He did manage to get stung several times for his effort, though. Still, he was not deterred and his eyewitness testimony would go a long way to convincing a jury of the truth.

Sam would have much preferred to transport the prisoner in the usual way, pulled in a buggy or even a wagon, but the depth of the snow made such travel impossible. As he climbed onto Cutter, he glanced over at Horace who was being led out of the house by Bet with his hands still cuffed in front of him. Thankfully, they had dressed him, and over his clothes he wore a long, sweeping coat with a hood that looked to be made of lightly tanned animal hide. It was probably of Indian make, Sam noted, and therefore a stout guard against the elements.

"Colvin?"

"Sir?" the big man replied, coming up to the sheriff on his horse.

"Here's how this is going to work." Sam spoke loud enough that Horace would hear even if he didn't understand. "If you'd be so kind, set him up on here behind me, but with his back to me so his arm's won't get him into trouble by trying something foolish enough to make me shoot him dead."

Sam then produced a long leather strap with a buckle that he had found among the various tack in the stable and handed it to him.

"Then you belt him to me with this. Hopefully, it keeps him from falling off but if he does go, this way I can be sure to go with him."

"All right," Colvin said and he reached for Horace as Bet led the man down the front steps.

Sam watched the big man as he handled the family patriarch, for he knew that it would only take a moment for him to snap the madman's neck like a chicken. And he knew in that moment, Colvin wanted nothing more in the world than to do just that.

But Colvin tossed Horace over his shoulder, the madman's crown of wasps slipping from his head and falling into the snow. Then seated him upon Cutter's back just the way Sam had directed. He stretched the leather strap around them and Sam took to pulling it tight before he buckled it.

With that done, the sheriff looked over the family who had gathered there for this miserable sight.

Bet and Twig mulled around at the edge of the group as they seemed given to do. While Charlotte stood with her arms folded at the base of the steps, sternly looking on, Lucy sat at the top next to Seena, her hands in her lap and that numbed look still in her eye. As for Charlotte, Sam could not discern if her dour expression betrayed anger toward him or if it was all directed at her father—maybe a little of both.

It grieved him. Nevertheless, he was in the business of catching criminals and Horace Crownhill sure as Hell was such a thing.

"Well," he sighed, "I reckon we better get a move on."

The family stirred but said nothing.

He clucked and Cutter began to move forward, down the hill in the direction of the trail he had come in on. As the crow flies, the trip would be much quicker through the woods than taking the main road that wound its way back to Selburn. So with precious little daylight left, that was where they headed.

"Sam?" he heard Charlotte call out and turned to see. "Do come back and see us."

He could tell it in the way that she wove her fingers together and then straightened her dress, those fingers that had run through his hair and over his body, that dress that had lain crumpled on the floor of the guest house only hours before. She said *us* but what she meant was *her*.

He tipped his hat and hoped she could see in his eyes that he would return, that he would be counting the moments until he could. These were not words he could speak in front of the others.

After a few minutes, the house disappeared behind the hill and they entered the woods along the southern edge of the estate.

"Horace, I just want you to know that if you get it in your head to try anything, I'll gutshoot you and leave you to die out here, nice and slow. Might even still be alive when the buzzards come for your eyes."

Sam bristled a little at his own words, wondering where that had come from, but he knew. Leaving the Crownhill house behind, he hoped to feel that oppressive presence lifted but as they entered into the wood, he could feel it even more.

It was ever-present and burdensome, like chains dragging behind them.

An hour passed and they had gone just over three miles by Sam's reckoning. The going on Cutter was sluggish with the old gal moving slower than usual due to the extra passenger on her back. That and having to slog through the snow that, when passing through shallow ravines, was so deep as to graze her belly.

All the while, the newly apprehended Horace Crownhill sat behind the sheriff, babbling often with the occasional outburst of mad laughter, like someone who had gotten something funny into his head and couldn't get it out.

"I wonder, Horace," Sam said, "just when that last tether to sanity withered away and you went so…well, my Da…he would have called you *barmy*."

He couldn't even be sure that Horace understood he was being spoken to. He grimaced. How was he ever going to put this lunatic on trial? He suspected that the man's attorney would make much hay of his condition and how he simply could not be held accountable for the actions of his clearly addled mind.

The breeze picked up and whistled through the trees. Snow fell from limbs above in great clumps and sheets, crashing to the forest floor. These were the only sounds they had for company, for there wasn't so much as a foraging squirrel to be glimpsed anywhere. These hushed woods were too still for Sam and he could not wait to be rid of them and back in Selburn proper. He longed for the warmth of the police station. Deputy Smyth would have a fire going surely. Sam also couldn't wait to hear the sound of the iron cell slam shut and see Horace Crownhill inside of it.

As they rounded a stand of thick pines, Sam's skin went tight with gooseflesh and he noticed Cutter's withers trembling and her ears pinned back. That was when it came—the white-devil wind, rushing all around them, stirring up snow and whipping into a painful, swirling storm. Sam did not take it for some mere weather anomaly this time, though. He had seen too much at Evermore to be so skeptical. Lowering his hat and bowing his head, he strived to calm Cutter beneath him, who stomped and shimmied, tossing her head back and forth, snorting in protest of the thing. What would his father do, he wondered?

Pray.

He was sure that his Da would have found some psalm or verse aimed at dispelling the presence of evil but all Sam could think of was the Our Father. Still, it was worth a shot.

"Our Father who art in Heaven, hallowed be Thy name..." he began. The wind seemed to worsen then, as if fighting back.

At the same time, behind him, Horace cackled wildly, raising his arms to the sky.

Cutter was in full panic now, high-stepping backward away from the devil wind.

"...on earth as it is in Heaven. Give us this day our daily bread..."

Sam bent down to stroke the old girl's neck, willing her to calm. The strap binding he and Horace together strained as he did.

Easy, now. Easy, he whispered in his mind, hoping that the horse could pick up on his will the way she so often did.

"...not into temptation but deliver us from evil. For thine is the Kingdom and the power..."

She would not be calmed, though, and she went stumbling backward, her backside cutting this way and that.

Afraid they would be pitched over the side, Sam doubled down and held the reins tight. He had barely gotten to the "Amen" when they were—all of them—falling as Cutter's hooves slipped on snow and rock. Being pinned beneath her would only make a bad situation worse so he pushed as hard as he could to launch himself and Horace from her back as she went down.

They came down in the snow together, a heap of flailing arms and hooves, strained cries and a guttural whinny of distress from Cutter herself. Pleased with having knocked them down, the devil wind eased up and Sam rolled to the right to see Cutter getting her legs back, though she was no less panicked.

He would need to get to her but with the burden of Horace attached to him it was impossible. He unbuckled the strap, letting it go slack and fall free as he jumped up and approached the mount with care.

"Come on, girl," he said. "Stand easy, it's over now."

And indeed it may well have been over, the wind dying to a breeze now, but it was not over for Cutter, whose wide eyes reflected a deep and abiding terror. What had she seen in the swirling white of that evil wind, he wondered?

But Sam would have to ask her later, for the horse whipped around and went tearing off, kicking and bucking into the vast woods, snow flying in her wake.

"Damn it," he shouted, tearing his hat from his head and tossing it aside.

He growled in disgust. Although she had run off in a huff, he knew the old nag would not get far before that burst of energy wore out, so catching up to her was not a concern. What vexed him more was the thought of having to trudge through the snowy wood with the madman in tow.

"Well, Horace, I hope you're up for a walk in the woods, old boy."

He turned and saw the man lying face down in the snow near an exposed rock where they had fallen, the old bastard not moving. As he tramped through the white toward him, he noted that the air felt warmer than it had even a few moments ago and a glance up at the sky led him to think the clouds may soon dissipate. How fine it would be to see blue sky again!

"Horace," he called as he came up next to the man and nudged him with his boot.

No movement.

Sam saw that the base of the exposed boulder was littered with other smaller rocks, most of them topped with a layer of snow, and he wondered if the old man hadn't cracked his head on one of them when they fell. He knelt down and grabbed him by the shoulder, turning him over.

The long whiskers of Horace's beard were packed with snow but as he came to rest on his back, the old man's eyes snapped open and a smile of delight spread across his face. The sheriff never even saw it coming when the old man's arm swung upward from the ground, a rock the size of a loaf of bread grasped in his bony hand.

It struck Sam on the side of the head and he went down in a blast of agony and blackening vision. He lay there a moment on his back as the world faded in and out, the gray of the winter light indistinguishable from the gray of unconsciousness that was quickly overcoming him. The old man was up, though, and crunching away through the knee-high snow. Sam managed to snatch his pistol from its holster, aim and fire a shot or two that missed their mark.

Spent, the sheriff's body gave out and he found himself lying face up in the snow, watching the drab canopy of clouds overhead as bits of proper sky began to peek through. The gray gave way to blue and then the blue gave way to black as the sky and the forest and the world faded from view.

CHAPTER 9
PURSUIT

Sam might have been out longer had he not rolled over in the midst of a lover's dream, thinking he would nuzzle into Charlotte's thick, blond hair again only to be greeted with the stinging, wet cold of snow on his face.

He sat upright and as his senses struggled to recover, he looked to the sky to see the blue but instead saw the bright pinpoints of stars spread overhead. Hanging among them, the white and waxing face of the moon shone down on the world below, painting the forest in stark, monochromatic contrasts. Getting to his feet, he patted his side. Remembering that he had gotten off a shot or two at the old man as he fled, he reached down into the snow and plucked the cold length of steel from it. Standing there, wavering, he considered his next course of action. Cutter was still missing and the fact was that Sam was much closer to Evermore than Selburn. Besides, that was likely where the old villain had run off to anyway. He scanned over the snowy ground and then marched farther into the woods, following the tracks of both his horse and his prisoner.

It was plain that several hours separated him from Horace but if the man held any memory of his land in the addled recesses of his mind, he could be warming himself by a fire in the manor house even now. If that were the case, and as long as he could find Cutter, Sam would spend one more night at Evermore and start out in the morning again. This time, though, he vowed that he would make Horace Crownhill walk all the way to Selburn if for no other reason than to watch the man suffer.

Time passed and the night deepened. Sam's pocket watch—the one that Da had carried and had famously deflected a bullet meant for his heart during a gunfight—had given up the ghost as he lay sleeping in the snow. How long he had been wandering the forest like a gypsy was anyone's guess but in the time he had done so, the warmth of the air caused a fog to rise above the snow. It became so thick that the tracks of Cutter's hooves disappeared, but still he labored forward in the general direction of them. He cursed the snow and the mist as he went and then, out of the corner of his eye, he saw something move among the trees.

Sam stopped and crouched down, watching.

He hoped to see the outline of his horse but what moved yonder was a man, his shape draped in light-colored fabric like the animal hide of Horace's coat. Beyond that, it was merely a white shadow that slipped through the trees far ahead, appearing and disappearing in the fog. It drifted over the snow, noiseless and upright.

"Horace, you old shit," the sheriff seethed, whispering the words.

He drew his pistol and cocked the hammer back.

At the moment, Horace seemed unaware of Sam, who knelt in the snow, watching. Hollering at the man to stop would only put him on alert and send him running off, and—quite frankly—Sam was not up to leaping through the snow to catch him.

The figure lingered in a dead, open space between the trees. The sheriff's trigger finger itched.

He could kill him right now—the thought came hissing into his mind. He could plug the nasty old shit and watch him bleed out and when the time came to account for it, no one would question the decision of Sheriff Sam Lock to pull on an escaped prisoner.

Sam breathed, turning the idea over, the pleading voice in his mind building.

Just like Paul Gentry, it whispered. *Mouth wide open at the end, drowning in the stew of his own brains.*

The sheriff recoiled from himself, his lip curled in disgust at his own thoughts. But had those notions been his own or had they been the urgings of whatever black presence dwelled here among the hills and fields? He holstered his pistol and crept through the snow, following the white figure as it drifted among the trees of the wood.

A structure in the wood emerged from the mist. Settling into the shelter of a stand of nearby pines, Sam looked on and watched as the white shape of Horace stopped and stood in place before it. The mist was thick and Sam was at first unable to comprehend the pale shadows of the leaning building but then, glancing around at the surrounding woods, he realized where it was the madman had come. And he could guess why easily enough.

It was the ramshackle remains of the tobacco barn that stood before him. On the other side, as if spellbound, there stood the figure in white, the old man drawn to the scene of his horrendous crime.

Sam hunkered down where he was and looked on. That field of debris was between himself and Horace, so he couldn't go dashing up ahead to tackle the man. However, he could round the barn and the debris and come upon him from the other side.

A stiff breeze rose up, flowing through the trees out of the east and the hood that covered the figure's head was tossed backward. In the pale light of the night, Sam could make out something atop Horace's head…something thin and wiry.

The crown of wasps. The very one that had fallen from the madman's head that morning and that Sam left lying there in the snow at the front entrance of Evermore.

Then, in the skies above, the moon emerged from behind a bank of clouds and the landscape of white was awash in an effusive, lunar glow. The breeze was still funneled through the trees and served to clear the fog that hovered over the snow. As it dissipated, Sam got a much cleaner view of the figure standing before the barn.

Pallid skin, as cold and fragile as fine china; a wire crown of dead, frozen insects set atop a head of long, golden locks that stirred with the breeze; and the eyes, dead eyes that Sam would have sworn were as black as pitch.

Could it be?

He gasped and stumbled backward into the evergreen brush, losing his footing and slipping to his bottom. As he scrambled back up, he hoped the rustling had not been heard. When he looked again at the figure, in the new light from the moon Sam could see an awful grin creep across those delicate features. A heartless shine of admiration it was, as a fond memory was revisited there before the wide, crimson stain that remained frozen in the snow where the young man was killed.

Unbelieving of what he was witnessing, Sam's rational mind fought against him. It offered other reasons for what he saw, plucking against his heartstrings to convince him of some other truth. In the end, there was only one way to know.

Sam took one final look at the figure, standing there in the ghostlight of the moon with that look of perverted delight, and the eyes that had been utterly black only a moment ago now returning to the piercing blue of a clear winter sky. Although, in a way, Sam reflected, the fascination and pride that he saw there revealed a truth of the heart—that if there was one still beating in her chest, it was as black and twisted and unrecognizable as her father's mind.

Scolding himself for having fallen victim to her practiced deception, he turned and made his way quietly through the wood to the north end of the property. There he expected to find the manor house dark and quiet with sleep and the lady of the Crownhill house missing from her bed.

CHAPTER 10
REVELATIONS

Entering through the servant's door into the kitchen, Sam found a lantern and lit it, then made his way through the still darkness of the house. Careful to preserve the silence, he moved slow and stepped lightly, ascending the main stairs like a specter. At the top, he turned and crept down the hallway to a door that stood ajar.

Inside, the sheriff pushed the door closed and turned to survey the room. The bed sheets and blankets had not been disturbed but there was a depression on the edge of the mattress where it looked as if someone had sat for a great while.

Sat doing what? he wondered.

Sam turned to align himself with the depression in the bed, trying to put himself in her shoes. Charlotte had sat here, looking into the fire, perhaps? But the fire in the room was cold and smoldering and the bed warming pan that leaned next to it looked unused.

On the bedside table there was a candlestick and matches, a silver hairbrush and hand mirror sitting atop a lace doily and a tablecloth which hung down nearly to the floor—nothing of particular interest. As he turned to move toward the fireplace, though, Sam's eyes fell on a series of small stains that marred the otherwise stark white fabric.

He leaned closer and held his lantern to it.

Dark stains. Droplets and a faint smear as if someone had at first tried to rub the stains out but then realized that would only make it worse. The blood—for Sam was certain that it was blood—had been allowed to set in and to seep down into the cotton fibers. Looking over the night table, he glimpsed something peeking out from beneath the edge of the tablecloth. Pulling the cloth aside, he picked a jewelry box up from the floor and set it on the bed.

In the foyer downstairs, the clock struck one hour past midnight.

It was a plain, square box of ebony wood with bone inlays in a diamond pattern. The lid was held in place by a lock which required a small key to open it. But Sam saw no such key anywhere near the table.

He considered for a moment what he should do next, though he knew it perfectly well. There was no force in this world that could stop him from prying that jewelry box open to find what he suspected was inside.

But he was no longer alone in the room.

"Sheriff," he heard her voice call to him, as the door creaked gently open, "do you mind telling me what you're doing in this room?"

He sighed and turned toward her.

Charlotte stood in the doorway, her peach-colored nightgown with ivory lace was ruffled, though neither her hair nor face betrayed having just woken from a night's rest. She had, of course, been awake for some time.

"I was hoping that you could tell me," he said, his face stern as he regarded her, "what is in this box and where I might find the key."

They stood there, staring at each other for a long moment before she offered a reply.

"What are you doing *here*?" Charlotte asked. "Shouldn't you be in Selburn locking my father away?"

"Your father," Sam mused. "The old fool cracked me in the head with a rock and ran off hours ago."

She blinked, her brow furrowing.

"Well, no one here has seen him," she offered.

Sam grimaced. Enough about the lunatic. In all likelihood, by now Horace Crownhill was out there frozen dead in the woods somewhere and good riddance to him.

"What's in the box, Charlotte?"

Her distracted gaze turned back to him and she shrugged.

"Why, jewelry, I should think."

He nodded.

"Jewelry. I see. And the key?"

"I don't have it."

His eyes never left hers and his face soured with doubt.

"That's a shame," he said as he pulled back his coat and drew a knife from his belt.

"What are you—"

But he was no longer listening. He turned back to the jewelry box and dug the point of his knife into the thin space beneath the lid.

"Sam, that's private property," she protested behind him.

He pried up, feeling the lock strain inside the box—once more, twice more.

The lid popped open and then shut again with a crack and he set it back down on the bed as he sheathed his knife.

"I don't quite understand what's going on here," she said from behind him, her voice trembling and flustered.

The sheriff pulled the lid up and glanced down into the box. What he saw there should have filled him with such satisfaction as to move him to smile, but in truth, he had never in his life hoped so dearly that his instincts be proven wrong.

There were dried, crimson stains all over the handkerchief that the blade had been wrapped in. He pulled the edges back to reveal the curved handle of a folding razor, crusted with smears of old blood.

Sam noticed then that Charlotte had come to stand beside him and as she looked down into the box, she gasped.

"What is this?" another voice asked and both Charlotte and Sam turned to see Lucy standing in the doorway, a long, fur coat just like her grandfather's hanging unbuttoned from her shoulders and nothing else underneath. "What are you and the sheriff doing in *my room*, Mother?"

Charlotte was stunned into silence. Sam looked Lucy up and down. Her feet and legs were bare and red from the cold and thick clogs of snow still stuck between her toes. Atop the girl's head sat one of her grandfather's homemade adornments with the tiny black and yellow shapes impaled upon it.

"Lucy?" Charlotte asked as if she wasn't entirely certain.

Sam reached down and pulled the razor from the box. Keeping it wrapped in the handkerchief, he thumbed open the blade. One side had been neatly inscribed with the name and location of the manufacturer; *John Barber, Sheffield*. On the blade's other side, crudely scratched into the metal in wild, angular strokes now filled with William's blood was a single word.

MAMMON.

Sam glanced over at the girl, thinking of how she had seemed when he saw her standing there by the old barn leering at the kill site, the smile on her face and the inhuman blackness of her eyes. He turned the blade over in his hand. Sam's father had been a deeply Christian man and he had endeavored to raise his son to have the same fiery faith as he. It hadn't taken, but the many lessons of the Old Testament were still with him, so he knew the name well enough. Mammon: one of the seven princes of Hell and champion of greed.

Charlotte was moving toward her daughter but Sam stopped her. He stepped forward, holding the razor up in his fingers. As she looked upon it, Lucy did not stammer for explanations or feign ignorance. In fact, Sam noted, the girl showed no reaction at all. She just stood there in the doorway, holding his gaze with that same dead look in her eyes that he had seen earlier that day when they discovered Mary's body hanging from the third floor balcony.

Poor Mary, Sam thought and narrowed his eyes, looking down to the young girl's hands. He lurched forward and grabbed one, pulling her arm out straight and pushing the sleeve of her coat up to reveal the fresh, red welts of stings up and down her skin in such number that even Charlotte could see them from where she sat on the edge of the bed.

Sam's eyes scanned over them and his mind worked as all the pieces began falling into place. He had been wrong all the while—so wrong.

"Did Horace help you?" he asked. "Did he help you hang that poor girl? Did he help you kill William, too?"

She curled her lip and raised her chin, proud and defiant.

"Grandfather didn't have the stomach for what I did," she said. "He stayed in his bed pretending to sleep while I marched her out to the balcony."

Sam dropped her arm and glared at her, circling her, studying her. She seemed nothing like the poor wilted flower that he had taken her for during his stay at Evermore.

"Why kill Mary?" he asked her.

She shrugged, dismissive.

"Why not?" she replied.

Charlotte flinched at the sting of the girl's cruel words.

Sam found his gaze drawn to the makeshift crown she wore. Impossibly, the still forms of the insects were moving again, their tiny wings flitting as they struggled to free themselves.

He tried to blink the sight away and turned his attention back to the girl's cold eyes.

"And William? Did he slight you in some way? Were the two of you in an argument?"

"Slight me?" she said, then scoffed. "That cornpone *peasant* was in love with me. Always fawning over me, sniffing around the hallway by my room, hoping to catch me changing clothes." She chuckled. "After the party, I told him that I had a birthday gift for him," she continued. "One that I could only give him in private…"

"What was the gift?" Sam asked.

She smiled.

"That I'd let him put his dirty little thing inside of me," she hissed. "After that, he would have done anything I told him to." She snorted a laugh. "It was pathetic."

Appalled and now fuming, Sam shook his head in disbelief.

"Tell me, Lucy," he shouted at her, "did you slice his prick to ribbons before or after you pushed him onto the blade of that reaper?"

Lucy stepped to the sheriff, who halted his circling as she placed her hand on the crotch of his pants, squeezing tightly.

"I cut it once," she whispered with venom, "while he was lying there with the blade stuck in him, and he screamed so loud that I couldn't help myself. So I cut him again and again."

Sam slapped Lucy's hand away and stepped back, revolted. The expression on the girl's face while telling of her foul deed was a likeness that he had seen on the face of her mother, though it had been while in the throes of passion. It sickened him to see it on the girl now.

That this demure young lady…this child…could be capable of such heinous and evil acts, he could not believe. Sam wanted to shut it out of his mind, all of it. But there it was in front of him, irrefutable, the girl stalking around him now like a predator.

Behind him, Charlotte made a whimpering noise, her hand going to her mouth. She looked to Sam as if she were about to be sick.

"What?" Charlotte breathed. "She did what?"

That's right, Sam thought. *She doesn't know.*

He hadn't revealed to her the full extent of what had been done to William.

"I asked your man, Colvin, not to tell you about the mutilation of William's body," Sam explained to Charlotte. "Frankly, considering his loyalty to you, I'm surprised that he didn't."

He turned back to Lucy and was about to continue when Charlotte was suddenly up and flying past him. With a wild swing, she smacked her daughter across the face and they fell into each other, Lucy fighting back and the two of them grappling as they careened across the room. Sam sidestepped their oncoming rush and the mother and daughter crashed into the bed and sank to the floor, pulling the sheets and the jewelry box down with them.

The sound of the ruckus had woken the servants. Sam could hear them coming down the hall. As he twisted around to call out to them, the door into the hallway slammed shut of its own accord. The knob turned and turned from the other side but the door would not budge. Sam could hear Bet's voice through the door.

"Miss Lucy? Miss Charlotte? Everything all right?"

The knob frantically twisted back and forth.

Across the room, the crown of wasps lay next to the hearth, the things impaled there still moving. Sam swallowed hard and looked away. All the air seemed to flush from the room and a sudden pressure filled his ears and head.

As the two women struggled, Sam felt unable to tear his eyes away from the wriggling insects on the crown. They should be dead, all of them. How could it be? Something preternatural was animating them.

There was banging on the door now and more voices from the hallway. A heavy fist that could only be Colvin's hammered against the wood.

The pressure rang in his ears and Sam thought of that blade with the devil's name scratched into it and, overcome with dread and fear, he wished only to sink into himself and diminish from all of this.

Mammon was here. Mammon had always been here.

Lucy let out a growl and pushed her mother away from her. The motion should have sent Charlotte backwards to the floor only feet away, but something more happened right before Sam's very eyes.

Charlotte sailed across the room and was thrust flat against the far wall. She remained there, unable to stand, unable to move, pinned against the wall by some unseen force. Her feet dangled inches above the floor. Lucy stood and regarded her mother with a dark amusement, then stepped slowly toward her.

The girl—if that's what she was anymore, if she had ever been—seemed unconcerned with Sam. Her ire and wrath was focused on Charlotte. It was an opportunity to stop this, to end this, and he needed to act.

Reaching down, deep into himself, steeling his mind against the fear that had consumed him so suddenly, Sam's hand went to his beltline and freed his pistol from its holster. He brought it up to aim at the girl as she crossed the room.

His throat was dry, so dry he felt it might close up, leaving him unable to breathe. He ran his tongue around behind his teeth, summoning some spit. He breathed a slow breath in through his nose and steadied his gun hand, cocked the hammer back.

Can I do this? he thought. *Can I truly do this...kill a child?*

But she wasn't just a child, was she? Lucy was something more, something monstrous. She'd become a vessel, a host for a dark power that had settled into her mind, into the blood and bones of the girl.

There had to be some other way, he reasoned. Enough blood had been spilled here. He needed time, they needed time. Time to find another way to bring the girl around.

Sam eased the hammer forward, then flipped the gun toward him, grasping it by the barrel. Summoning more will than he might have imagined necessary, he crossed the room with a quickness, straight toward Lucy.

He struck before she saw him coming. Bringing the gun back and past his ear like a hammer, he swung and the heavy grip caught the girl in the side of the head. She turned toward him, stumbled and he drew back again. This time, when he swung the weapon it smashed into her skull just behind her ear and slipped from his hand, going airborne across the room.

But the combined strikes had done the trick. Lucy's eyes rolled back in her head, her knees buckled, and she collapsed in a heap onto the floor. The girl and the entity inside of her had been rendered inert. Asleep, for the moment.

Charlotte abruptly dropped to the floor and Sam rushed over to her.

The air had returned and the pressure receded. Both Sam and Charlotte's chests heaved as they caught their breath.

"Are you all right?"

She gasped and coughed but nodded.

The door burst open and Colvin and Bet rushed in from the hallway. Behind them, Seena and Twig lingered in the doorway. Sam could see from the wild look in the old woman's eyes that she was loathe to enter.

"What's happened, Sheriff?" Colvin asked, looking over at Lucy crumpled on the hearth.

Sam heard the question well enough but had no answer. How could he explain what happened? Where would he even begin?

Kneeling there, Sam saw the jewelry box where he had found the blade tipped over. Something else had fallen out of it—three things to be precise. Three locks of hair, each bound at one end with a length of thread: one long and dark, its silky shine easily recognizable as Mary's; another dark and wiry, clearly having belonged to young William; the third, blond like Charlotte's but fine and soft—the hair of a child. A very young child.

He wondered if it was Lucy's own. But why keep such a thing in the box with the others that the girl regarded as mementos from the two murders?

Unless there had been another.

"Charlotte," he said, reaching over and picking up the yellow bit of hair, "who did this belong to?"

He thought of the crib and the toys he happened upon in the attic. Toys meant for a baby boy, but not for William. The woman looked over to him, her eyes filling with anguished tears that streamed down her cheeks.

"Let's get you out of here," he said, helping her to her feet.

He motioned for Bet and Colvin to come over.

"Take Miss Charlotte down to the parlor, please," he said. "She needs to rest."

They nodded and each hooked an arm beneath the woman's shoulders, helping her step gingerly down the hallway toward the stairs. Seena and Twig shuffled along with them, the old woman yawning as she went and the thin young man rubbing sleep from the corners of exhausted eyes.

Sam looked back at Lucy lying motionless on the floor.

Dear God, had he killed her after all?

A quick check of her pulse reassured him that he had not. He bent down and scooped the girl up and deposited her on the bed.

Sam recovered his pistol first, then the small locks of hair and the jewelry box, which he tucked under his arm, and stepped through the door. As he left the room, he glanced over to the hearth at the crown of wasps there. He was heartened to see the creatures as still and cold as they should be.

Appropriately dead.

Sam met Bet and Colvin coming back up the stairs, the big man's heavy iron peg leg thumping along as he came.

"What happened, Sheriff?" Colvin asked.

Sam placed a hand on his shoulder.

"I'll explain later," he said. "But right now, I need you to secure that door from the outside. Nail it shut, maybe. I don't know. But the thing in that room cannot be allowed to leave."

Colvin cocked his head to the side. "You mean Miss Lucy?"

Sam paused. "I suppose I do."

He left the other men to their task and hurried down the stairs to the parlor where he hoped the lady of the house would be resting comfortably.

When he entered, though, he found her pacing the room. She held a glass of whiskey in a trembling hand.

"Is she—"

"She's unconscious," he said. "But she's alive."

Charlotte nodded, though Sam was not sure if this news pleased her or not.

He set the jewelry box down on the table and watched as the woman's gaze was drawn to it. She sat down and opened it, fingering the lock of blond hair, turning it over and over.

"Shall we continue the conversation, Sam?"

He shook his head.

"Perhaps now is not the time for that."

"No," she said. "It's likely not. But it is important that you know."

"All right," Sam said and settled onto the couch next to her. "Then tell me."

Charlotte Crownhill explained that before her late husband, Lyle Neville, had died of consumption, they had been blessed with two lovely children—Nathan and his sister, Lucy, who was older than him by six years. Not long after Nathan's birth, Lyle fell sick. The consumption quickly devastated the poor man and he didn't live long enough to see his newborn son's first birthday. Lucy took the death of her father very hard and was often struck with debilitating fits of melancholia and bouts of uncontrollable anger. As time went on, the girl seemed to do better, although when baby Nathan suffered crib death at the age of eight months, Charlotte had been too distraught and mired in a malaise to notice that her young daughter was coping well with the devastating loss. Uncommonly well, in fact. Seena had noticed, though, and she told Charlotte of it one day, expressing concern at the girl's demeanor and a growing coldness she had seen in her.

"But I never..." Charlotte began, drifting off into quiet sobs.

Sam nodded. "You never imagined that she could have done something to Nathan."

"My baby...he was such a little...such a fragile thing," she sobbed. "How could Lucy...why would she?"

He sighed, shaking his head. She was far better qualified to answer that question than he was. Jealousy, perhaps, of the newborn made worse by the loss of her father. But that felt to him like an excuse and he had already been taken in by the young girl's charade all this time. He would not be taken in further. There was no answer in the world to satisfy Charlotte's question—none at all.

Charlotte poured another whiskey and sipped on it while Sam sat back and wondered at the awful truths that had been laid bare that night.

"Do you think she can be treated?" she asked.

He shrugged. "She's your child," he said. "You know her mind better than anyone. What do you think?"

Tears welled in her eyes. "I'm not sure, Sam," she said, her voice breaking, "that I know her mind at all. That I ever have."

After a moment, she continued. "Truthfully, ever since she was young, Lucy has always seemed oddly cruel. To people, to animals. We had a dog once, you know."

"That right?"

"A purebred Shetland. Harry was his name. A beautiful animal. In the cold months, he would sleep on the hearth by the fire."

Sam smiled. "That sounds nice."

"Lucy would sneak up on him," she said. "She would place embers from the fire on the hearth and edge them closer and closer to the poor thing. Sometimes his fur would burn long before the heat woke him and sent him running from the room, yelping all the way."

"Not so nice, then."

"But it's not just Lucy, is it? Something dark has gotten inside of her."

He nodded.

"All my life, I've heard them speak of it, you know…the servants, the workers here. Always in whispers. Some nameless evil that dwells here."

"But you never believed?"

She shook her head.

"Well," Sam said, "if you believe it now, there may be some hope for her."

"How so?"

"Are you a church-going woman, Charlotte?" he asked.

"I was raised Methodist."

"Well," he said, pouring a bit more whiskey into his glass, "my father was Irish. A Roman Catholic who raised me as such."

He sipped.

"The Roman church believes in dark spirits…demons, devils…and they have methods of dealing with such things. Ways to cast them out of a person."

Her brow wrinkled. "You're talking about exorcism? It's just superstitious nonsense, isn't it?"

"I would have said so, yes," he said, "but the things I've seen here, Charlotte…what we experienced just now in her room…have changed my mind."

"You're suggesting such a rite be performed on my daughter," she said. "But there are no Roman churches here in Selburn."

"No, but there is the Bethlehem chapel in town. It's an Anglican church and their priests know the rite as well."

He could hardly believe what he was suggesting. The girl was a murderess, after all.

"She'll need to answer for her crimes," he said. "But if she could be cured of the thing inside of her, perhaps…" he struggled for the words. It was a desperate idea and one which he knew nothing about aside from his father's tales of demon-haunted folk in the Irish countryside. "Perhaps the court might show some mercy and send her to a sanitarium."

Charlotte stood and went to the window, looking out upon the frozen landscape; bright white in the light of the moon.

"That's a strange suggestion coming from a sheriff."

He tried for a smile but managed something marginally better than a grimace.

"I'm suggesting it as a friend," he said. "I'll take her myself. Tomorrow. I'll make the arrangements and you can be there if you like."

She turned to him.

"Can I ask something of you, then? As a friend."

"Anything."

She set her glass down on the table.

"Hold me. If only for a moment."

For Sam, it was hardly a favor. He rose and went to her, folded her in an embrace. He laid his face against her neck. Buried it into the tangles of her golden hair and held her tight against him. God, the woman's perfume!

"Do it, then, Sam," she whispered in his ear. "Bring Lucy back. If she can be brought."

He nodded, though he was unsure of the possibility. Sam was still uncertain how many of the black deeds Lucy had done were influenced by the demon thing and how many had been the awful acts of a deranged mind, bent with cruelty and bloodlust.

Charlotte turned her face to him and brought her lips to his. They kissed, each of them searching for a deep and desperate comfort. The stillness of that moment and its quiet fire were shattered, though, with the sound of a great calamity above their heads. It echoed through the house and they withdrew from one another.

They had just made it past the parlor door when Sam saw Bet come running, his face long and his mouth agape.

"Something's happenin', Miss Charlotte," he said.

They all stood there a moment, dumbfounded as thunderous and repetitive noises beat down through the timbers from the room above. Lucy's room.

Then Sam was off, blazing through the foyer and up the stairs, Charlotte and Bet trailing behind him, passing Colvin and Twig along the way. Upstairs, the noise had drawn Seena out of Horace's chambers to gawk at Lucy's room at the end of the hall.

In the flickering light of the hall candles, Sam saw the door to the girl's room. Bet and Colvin had fixed it shut with a block of wood nailed into the door itself and to the threshold. The hammer and nails still lay on the floor. But the door was trembling violently against this restraint.

Beyond it there was a cacophony of random noises and a deep and terrible hum that Sam remembered all too well from his visit to Horace's third-floor chamber of madness.

"What's happening?" Charlotte cried out.

Sam looked back at her. "I think it's awake again."

Beyond Charlotte and Bet, at the end of the hallway, he saw Seena standing there. Her eyes went skyward and she made odd motions with her hands as she mumbled something in what Sam suspected was her native tongue. A prayer to some pagan god of the dark continent. Although he couldn't understand her words, he could guess their meaning well enough. Something evil lurked beyond the door and she was asking for protection against it.

He reached down, took up the claw hammer, jammed its curved edge between the block and the door and pulled.

As they were yanked from the wood, the nails groaned like tortured souls.

CHAPTER 11
THE SCREAMING DARK

When the last nail was removed, the passage into Lucy's bedroom swung open and slammed against the inside. Caught in the moment, Sam and Charlotte rushed in, heedless of the dangers that might lay beyond it.

Sam beheld the source of the terrible, crashing noise they had heard while down in the parlor. Lucy's chamber was located directly below the third-floor room where Horace had been staying and the joists between the two had been splintered with an ungodly force, opening the ceiling of Lucy's bedroom and spilling the contents of the room above into it.

The Wasp King's table, where he constructed his bizarre wares, lay on the girl's bed and timbers and walling littered the floor from the breach.

Lucy herself was away from the bed, rising into the air, borne by the demonic force within her. Likely the same force, Sam thought, that ripped the ceiling down. Suspended in the midst of the chaos, the girl twitched and shook such that Sam was sure it would have rapped and broken her bones.

Her head was bent back, her mouth opened wide, and from it there erupted a great and piercing scream that was not the voice of one but of legions of souls, pitched into darkness and anguish. And all about the room, objects flew in a whirlwind, smashing against each other, furniture and ephemera cast about in a storm.

At the hearth, the dying fire burned brighter than it should have, raging flames licking up the brick and blackening the mantel. And the crown of wasps was writhing once again, each of the insects given new and unnatural life.

Sam drew his pistol and aimed it at the floating girl.

Then came the first sting.

He hadn't noticed it until now but along with the contents of Horace Crownhill's room, the thousands of wasps he kept for company had been loosed. They zipped about through the air, lighting upon every surface, every person. Spilling through the door and into the rest of the house.

But Lucy was riddled with their crawling forms.

They clung to her like a second skin, a weird and undulating mass of sharp abdomens and clicking legs, beating wings that buzzed with a deafening resonance.

Sam slapped at the one that sank its stinger into his arm and saw Charlotte dancing madly before him, stubbornly endeavoring to get to her daughter in the storm of debris and insects.

"Lucy," she called out. "Lucy, come back to me."

To Sam, it seemed a pointless attempt, for nothing changed. Not the flurry of objects or the dark, air-sucking presence in the room.

"Jesus, save us!" Charlotte screamed. "Holy Spirit, send us your grace, for we are in need."

The flurry of objects slowed, many of them dropping to the floor.

"Yea, though I walk through the valley in the shadow of death—" Charlotte began reciting from the Psalms.

"I will fear no evil," Sam joined in.

He wouldn't have guessed that something so simple could be so effective, but by God it was working.

"For you are with me. Thy rod and thy staff, they comfort me," they chanted in unison.

The air seemed to still for a moment then and the girl looked down on her mother. Though he could not be sure, Sam thought he saw something of

Lucy—the true Lucy—wash over her persona as she descended gently, her feet touching the floor.

The wasps that had clung to her a moment ago were lifting off, buzzing away to their nests in the ceiling and rafters of the attic room above.

"You prepare a table before me in the presence of my enemies—" Charlotte continued.

"Mommy?" she said, cutting in.

Charlotte waved against the blizzard of wasps, making her way toward her daughter.

"Baby?" she asked in a fragile and forlorn voice, her arms outstretched.

Lucy accepted her mother's embrace and closed her eyes, going slack, weary as she was.

"Mommy?" she said again.

Sam swatted at the few wasps that still flitted about but mostly they passed him by with little interest, the great tumult at long last over.

He looked on with a dawning sense of hope, although some dismal part of him knew that the girl would have to spend many nights in the Selburn jail before it was all over.

Charlotte held her daughter close and stroked the girl's long, yellow hair.

"Did you like it, Mommy?" he heard Lucy whisper into her mother's ear.

Questioning, Charlotte cocked her head and smiled.

"Did you like when the sheriff was inside of you, you whoring cunt?"

Sam heard the words and, without hesitation, raised his gun to aim at the girl's head not five feet away.

But the servant wasps had returned and were on him again, this time in full force, stinging his hands and neck and every bit of exposed flesh they could light upon. With his free hand, he swatted at them but to no avail.

"I hated it, Mother," Lucy spat, holding Charlotte close. "Hated the nigger boy's thing in my mouth."

Sam saw the flash of the razor in the young girl's hand as she pressed it against Charlotte's nightgown, MAMMON emblazoned on the one side. In the aftermath of the previous attack on Charlotte, he had overlooked it. Understandable perhaps but no less unforgivable.

"But I did it for you, Mother," Lucy hissed. "To be *just like you*."

He cursed his own stupidity and pulled the trigger, but with the dozens of wasps plunging their stingers into his gun arm, the shot went wild and blasted harmlessly into the wall as the pistol dropped to the floor.

Lucy jabbed the razor into Charlotte's guts and ripped it across, leaving her mother in a screaming, blood-darkened pile. When he finally mustered the wherewithal to intercede, the murderess stretched a hand out toward Sam and sent him flying against the far wall where his head snapped to the side and met with the sharp corner of the fireplace mantel.

Sam went limp and slid to the floor.

The room blurred. A black tunnel emerged from nowhere and pulled him deep. Stars swam across his vision and the last thing he saw before the engulfing blackness was Lucy, draped in wasps, drifting through the door toward Bet.

CHAPTER 12
CHAMBERS OF DREAM

He stood in a wide, grassy meadow. The shafts and tips, elbow high, rippled in the mountain breeze, an ocean of undulating green. God Almighty, it was peaceful. Sam closed his eyes, sought to drift away.

Somewhere behind him, the crack of a gunshot pierced the tranquil rustle of the meadow in the wind. Sam turned to see that old good-time brothel that would forever occupy a place high in his mind, perched like a dark tower over his consciousness.

But he wasn't conscious, was he?

He grazed his fingers over the grass tips and felt them. Bristled, seedy things they were, and they felt real enough. But this meadow was no place, no place he knew. Certainly not where the brothel had been.

Another shot rang out from the brothel, borne across to him on the wind.

Sam stepped into the sea of grass between him and the house, taking slow and plodding steps. He didn't want to go there, not really. But he felt he must. There was something there he needed to see.

As he came up on it, he stared up into the windows, many broken, many missing, others that had been intact now shot out. The house was splintered, ravaged by the storm of bullets the bad men had brought down upon it. But they were nowhere to be found.

The boards groaned as he stepped onto them. Just above, on the porch, was the woodpile and Sam knew very well that his father lay behind that woodpile, dead and covered red from all the blood he had coughed up in his final moments.

Except he wasn't there.

Sam gawked at the absence of his old man, the absence of any trace of the blood and death he had seen there last, so many years ago.

A noise came drifting out of the house, a high-pitched squeal—the kind made by a child young enough to still be in their nappies.

"Better get in there, boy," Sam heard his father say.

He turned back to the woodpile and found him there this time, limbs twisted in agony, torn and broken as a rag doll. He stared up at Sam with death-white eyes and when he spoke, his dry lips looked like they might crack, his teeth stained crimson behind them.

"Better see what she's been up to," his father wheezed. "What *it's been up to*."

The door was hanging open just the way Sam remembered it. He had crawled past it on his way up to that bedroom where he had left his pistol. Where he had hidden while they shot his father to death.

In the room past the door, there were no bodies but plenty of evidence they had once been there. Furniture was overturned, rugs flipped up and askew. There were bloodstains everywhere Sam could put his eyes. Red swipes on the doorways where red hands had tried to steady themselves, seeking refuge and escape from the men that walked the house that dark morning, dealing death to all.

Sam looked away but as he stepped into the next room, he tripped over something and fell. A body, small and mechanical. The crawling doll with its mutilated face, moving past him toward a dark corner of the dream.

He rolled and got to his elbow to stand. As he did, he saw between two ragged old couches near the door, saw to the far wall and the busted window that hung there, jagged remnants of glass still clinging to the pane. Outside of the window, young Mary's face greeted him, her neck bent at that terrible angle. Behind her, the metal wire was still taut and she swung gently back and forth. Her lips moved and whispered something he could not hear.

The sight of her sent his heart racing, though, and he scrambled to his feet, proceeding into the next room.

But he was no longer in the brothel, not really. The rooms he remembered from that rambling house had melded with the ornately furnished rooms of Evermore, and where there should be the front hallway, instead he found the parlor room with its mahogany chairs and silver candlesticks.

Charlotte sat in a chair along the far wall, draped in the funeral attire of a widow. Her face was lost behind the black veil, where she sobbed continuously. In the center of the room, in her nightgown, stood Lucy. Her back was to him and she paid his presence there no mind.

She stood by a crib that Sam recognized right away.

In one hand she held a blanket. In the other, the razor.

Sam watched, detached, helpless. There was nothing he could do. He was there to bear witness, nothing else.

She raised the blanket to cover the child inside the crib but paused, then crushed the blanket into a tight ball that looked like a boulder in her grasp. She leaned in and the cries and squeaks of her little brother were quickly muffled.

Sam's father was beside him then, a walking nightmare on two legs.

"See what she's done? All the things?"

He nodded.

"I see, Da. I know."

A moment passed, maybe two. The child's cries ceased and there was nothing to be heard but Charlotte's mournful wails from across the room.

Lucy reached into the crib with the razor and pulled back a swatch of the fairest, finest hair Sam had ever laid eyes on. Like slivers of gold gleaming in the amber light of sunset.

He shut his eyes against it.

"I've seen enough," he said, then turned and stormed past his father.

He wanted out of the house, off the porch. He would return to that unknown meadow, wherever and whatever it was, and there he would stay for all time.

"Like Hell ye've seen enough," he heard his old man whisper behind him.

Sam had just stepped back into the other room when he felt a cold hand on him. Icy and strong, it spun him around and he was closer to his father's ruined face than he cared to be.

"The devil knows no redemption," he spat at him.

Sam tore away and stumbled back into the room but it was not what it was a moment ago. The open door was not there, the porch nowhere in sight. It was a small room, undecorated, stinking of piss and sweat and sex.

A room with a single bed that he knew all too well.

His father still stood behind him. He could feel the cold of his presence.

Sam looked long at that bed, trembling, wondering if he was about to see himself come crawling out from under it. A cowardly bug slipping from beneath its protective rock now that the predator had passed by.

But the bed was not empty. The top sheet had been replaced by a filthy canvas tarpaulin, beneath which something lay. Something dreadful. Sam was sure of it.

"Go on, son," he heard his father say. "See for yerself."

He shook his head but found himself moving closer to the bed, reaching out a hand toward the cover.

"It won't matter," he said. "She's only a child. They can help her. The priest, maybe."

"The dark thing's been inside her so long, Samuel, there's no tellin' them apart anymore."

Sam reached out and pulled back the canvas.

William lay there, unmoving but alive. It shocked him to see the color returned to the boy's flesh, the liveliness of his entire form. He gasped with surprise and went to touch William's leg but found his hand was not empty.

Grasped in it was the ivory handle of the Sheffield razor, the scars of the demon's name carved into its blade, leering at him.

It was strange and confusing. The hand was not his own. He glanced to the side where a faded mirror hung on the wall, and saw that it was not his own face reflecting back. Instead, he saw through Lucy's eyes, wrapped in Lucy's skin and clothes.

She leaned forward and took the boy's hardened prick into her mouth, sliding up and down, edging the blade along his thigh, ever closer. Inside of Lucy, Sam reeled and gasped, wanting nothing more than to flee this body and this room.

Most of all, he wanted to be rid of the feelings. Lucy's feelings. The sheer delight that was slipping over her as the red, red moment approached.

"Does she feel like a bloody child to ye, Samuel?" his father called out to him, his voice sharp with rage. "Does she?"

The blade flashed and slipped through the soft skin of the boy's private bits like butter and the screams flowed as free and terrible as the blood. The air was soaked with the sensuality of the violent act and the blade in his hand returned to the flesh again and again, stripping it with slow strokes as the boy, motionless, howled in pain.

Then something broke and Sam felt himself slip from her, slip out of her and into his own self again. He turned and ran from the room, turned the corner and met with another chamber of the dream.

Snow crunched beneath his feet and the chill wind bit into him. Looking about, he saw only a vast expanse of trees and night. In the sky above, stars twinkled. Sam tried to recognize something but he carried with him no lantern and the forest, so far as he could see, was unending and featureless. He moved forward, figuring some direction to be better than none.

As he loped along through the deep snow, he looked often to his side. From the corner of his eye, he kept seeing movement. Something pacing him, following as he meandered aimlessly through the woods.

A shadow passing between trees.

He stopped and watched, silent. When the shadow appeared again, he called out but it gave no reply.

"Da?" he hollered. "What is this? Why do you torment me?"

It's not a torment, he heard the old man's voice in his mind.

He blurted out a peel of mad laughter and trudged onward, snow spraying up as he plunged his legs down.

"Ain't it? Then what have you come for, Da?"

This all felt too familiar. Sam had had quite enough of wandering the woods around Evermore. He'd had his fill of all of it. Not for the first time since he came here, it felt as though he was drowning slowly, mired in ghosts and death and secrets, all of them pulling him low.

If he didn't break their grip soon, his mind would be ravaged and he would surely succumb to this awful place. That or the snow would take him. He was quaking inside his skin from the chill.

It's a warnin', his father replied after a moment. *Always been a warnin', leadin' up to this.*

Sam stopped, not only because of his father's words but because he saw something ahead that he knew did not belong there. In the inky night of the forest, he saw an amber glow. It trembled and shimmered. The light of a fire. The promise of warmth.

He took his steps forward carefully then, as quiet as he could. The closer he got to it, the more he saw. Nestled against a small hill was a pile of stones. At first glance, they seemed randomly placed but as Sam drew nearer, he saw they were not. Though he had no idea where anyone had gotten so many of them, they were piled up against the hill to create a small landing of some kind. Set before it, a great fire burned.

Sam's mind bid him to be cautious but his chattering teeth and bones sent him barreling forward toward the flames and the comfort they promised. He tore through the snow and when he erupted into that small clearing, the snow having been melted down to nothing by the fire's heat, he nearly stepped into the roaring conflagration.

As he stood there, basking in the glow and rubbing his hands together hungrily at the licking flames, he felt sated. Smoke billowed toward the cold stars above and the firelight rendered the woods as tall, looming shadows dancing to and fro, stepping side to side like the many legs of an enormous and inhuman beast. Only then did he see the pile of rocks against the hillside for what it was.

A great, crude chair of mossy, vine-covered stone. And on that chair sat one final horror.

Horace, the Wasp King, sitting there upon his throne, robed in crawling insects. His crown rested atop his head but the man was not as whole as he had been when Sam had seen him last. His naked flesh was pale and thin and marred, the patriarch seeming more like a corpse than a living man.

And his eyes. Those horrible eyes. If Sam lived ten thousand days beyond this day, he would never forget the sight. Horace's eyes were gone. In their place, thick, frozen kudzu roots emerged from the dead sockets and curved upward and over his head, curling into points like the horns of Satan himself.

All around him, other roots that had snaked up between the rocks grew upon the man, holding him in place. In the Wasp King's right hand, he held a goblet of weathered, rusted metal. Not filled with wine or spirits, it brimmed with hundreds of his insectile servants. They clicked and buzzed over each other as the King grinned, raised a toast to Sam and then turned it up, emptying them into his mouth.

The Wasp King smiled at him, all the tiny creatures swimming out from between his lips and covering his face so completely that, in an instant, there was nothing left of the man beneath. Nothing but the wild roots where his blue and maddened eyes should have been in that mask of a thousand humming insects.

Sam turned to run but his movement was heedless of his surroundings and the dangers, and he took a long step forward into the fire. At once, he was awash in its licking flames. His clothes burned and melded with his skin and all of it bubbled as a searing pain ripped through him from head to toe.

Beyond the fire, perched upon the rocks, the root-eyed Wasp King cackled as Sam diminished into the flames, becoming nothing more than cooked meat. With one last, feeble effort he lurched forward to escape but impaled his head on a sharp, white-hot log.

And the world fell away.

CHAPTER 13
FALLEN HOUSE, FALLEN SOULS

When Sam woke, he struggled through the thick residue of the dream toward consciousness, swimming toward that lone shore. Once he arrived and his mind cleared, he scurried off the hearth where he had landed, swatting at the flames that lighted along his pants leg from the roaring fireplace.

The room was, as he remembered, a shambles. But it was terribly quiet. As he rose up and looked around, getting his bearings, he saw Charlotte in the far corner, slumped against the wall, a hand to her stomach. It was dark and glistening from the wound her daughter had inflicted just before tossing him against the mantel.

He scrambled over the debris to her and found her alive and somewhat alert, shuddering and gasping with pain. He pressed his hands against her wet belly and searched the room. Lucy was nowhere to be found.

"I...I'm...all...all right," Charlotte stammered, doubled over.

She raised a limp hand toward the doorway, pointed, and Sam followed, getting to his feet.

Beyond the threshold, he found Bet lying across the hallway, his knees curled to his chest. The boy had stood his post even after what he had seen, had even tried to stop Lucy. And she had dealt him horrible blows. His face was a ruin, replete with lacerations from the Mammon blade. Sam wasn't certain and did not care to examine further but he thought he saw the boy's left eye dislodged from its socket and dangling just below his cheek. The old woman, Seena knelt beside him. She appeared unharmed but shaken, pressing rags against the young man's wounds.

Seena and Bet were both covered in welts from the stings of the wasps, just as Sam and Charlotte were. The stings rose on Sam's fair skin, red and burning and sore. He felt them on his face, dozens of them. Many of the damnable insects still buzzed about the house but the cold air was seeping in from the attic and slowing them. As Sam stumbled into the doorway and gawked at the sight, Seena looked up.

"Will he live?" he asked.

Seena glanced down at the boy and nodded slowly.

"How 'bout Miss Charlotte?" she asked. "She all right?"

He shook his head. "She may not live," he blurted out. "See to her, please."

He stepped over them and trod down the hallway to the upstairs landing. From that lofty vantage, he could see down into the candlelit foyer and what he saw spurred him onward. He wasted not a moment. Sam bounded down the stairs, taking them two at a time. His burned leg and body replete with stings protested greatly, but he gritted his teeth through the pain as the anger in him rose to such a level as to overtake it.

Earlier, when he and Charlotte had bolted up the stairs, Colvin and Twig had been standing there in the foyer, horror etched onto their faces as they listened to the ungodly noises overtaking the house from upstairs.

Now, though, as Sam rounded the post at the bottom, he saw only Colvin, who lay prone on the marble tile. The front door was wide open, the cold winter air seeping into the house, and Twig was nowhere to be seen.

He dashed over to Colvin and slid to his knees beside him. The big man was trying to right himself, inching along the floor on one knee, struggling to get up. Sam offered his hand but then saw the problem. The iron peg that was Colvin's other leg lay on the ground beside him. The leather straps that held it tight against his stump had been cut away, clean as could be. The leg beneath his pants was also crossed with lacerations and bleeding.

"Lucy?" Sam asked, placing a steadying hand on the man's shoulder.

Colvin nodded and grabbed at his sleeve as Sam made to get to his feet.

"I saw into her eyes, Sheriff," he said. "Saw into her proper."

"Yeah?"

Colvin twisted, looking wide-eyed toward the open doorway.

"It ain't Miss Lucy," he said. "Maybe it never was."

Sam nodded.

"It's all right, Colvin," he said.

He stared out through the open front door and felt his blood go cold. A chill breeze fluttered in. Beyond, the darkness beckoned. He feared that she—*that it*—was luring him out of the house, into the forest, and with the dream or vision so fresh in his mind, he did not wish to follow. Somewhere out in those woods was a roaring fire and by that fire sat Horace Crownhill, bound to his rooted throne, a deathless thing—eyeless and cackling at whatever Hell-borne sights the demon had cursed him with. No, Sam most certainly did not wish to follow.

"What about Twig?" he asked Colvin.

The big man began to speak but the battered, croaking sound of a young girl's voice interrupted.

"He's right here, Sheriff," it said.

Sam looked up and saw Lucy standing on the porch just beyond the doorway. She held Twig close to her, the Mammon blade pressed to his neck.

"It needs him, you know," she hissed. "To feed. It needs us all."

Sam leaned back and relaxed his posture. Inside his heart and his head, he was a shaking, terrified mess, but he could not betray that to the dark thing. Could not give it the pleasure or the advantage.

"All right," he said. "But why him?"

Her black eyes squinted.

"It needs what it needs and cares for nothing besides."

The blade pressed tighter against the boy's neck and a dribble of blood ran below its edge.

Sam slid his right hand down to his belt, feeling for the grip of his pistol. But he found only the softened edge of the empty leather holster.

Damn, he cursed himself. He had drawn it, fired it in her bedroom upstairs. Then the damnable wasps had set down upon him and he had lost all control.

Lucy regarded him, cocked her head at such an extreme angle that it reminded him of poor Mary hanging from the rear balcony.

"Oh," she frowned, theatrical in her mockery of sorrow.

When she spoke again, it was with the voice and Irish brogue of his father.

"Forgot yer steel again, did ye?" She snorted. "Ye bleedin' fuckwit!"

Hearing his father's words from her mouth surprised him a little, but he held her gaze, unblinking and deadpan in his stare.

Something moved in the darkness behind her. Sam's blood ran cold, certain that the Wasp King had returned from his exile in the wilderness, but a snort and a heavy crunching of snow told him it was only Cutter wandering back onto the grounds.

"Lucy," Sam said, "I want you to hear me."

She growled at him, pressed the blade closer to Twig's throat.

Twig sucked in a quick breath and his body shook as she held him against her with more paralyzing strength than a girl her size and age should have command of. But then it wasn't just her, was it?

An acrid smell swept in from the doorway and Sam saw a puddle forming below the boy's feet where he stood. So terrified was the young man that he had soiled himself.

"Lucy, it doesn't need his blood," Sam said.

It was all he could do not to lurch forward and attempt to stop her. But he knew he would be too slow and in those few seconds, she would slide the blade easily across the boy's throat and open the flesh.

"It does, it does, we do," she said, her words quick, one after another.

Sam straightened and made a show of his empty hands.

"Take my blood instead," he offered. "Take me."

He leaned forward on his hands, lowered his gaze in a gesture of supplication.

She cocked her head again.

"You offer *your life*," she said, seeming both amazed and amused, "for the life of this servile little brat?"

Sam said nothing, for the air had gone still. She rocked to and fro on her heels, considering.

It considered.

Sam glanced over at Colvin, who slowly shook his head.

"Ain't worth it, Sheriff," he whispered. "You're talkin' about your soul."

Sam nodded.

"Don't," the big man said.

Sam gave him a nervous, cockeyed smile. "It's all right," he whispered.

In one movement—a movement that Sam hoped would be swift enough—he grasped the discarded iron prosthetic of Colvin's leg and took it up, drew back over his head and thrust forward. He let go of the iron with all the force he could muster and watched as it whistled through the air, tumbling end over end, the leather straps flapping like the wings of a bird.

It struck Lucy squarely on the forehead, snapping her head back and sending her tumbling backward off the porch. The razor fell to the snow-covered brick of the porch. Twig crumpled, whimpering and crawling toward the door. Sam looked down at the boy as he stepped over him. If only he had time to comfort him, to soothe him.

But that was not his business.

When he found the iron peg in the snow, he took it up again and, for a moment, stood over Lucy, watching, weighing all that he had come to learn about the girl and about Evermore. The house's black secrets were eclipsed only by the blacker thing that held young Lucy in its thrall.

Lying there, helpless in the snow, she was a child. A smallish girl. Nothing more. But he knew in his heart what he could not reason through his eyes. In the dream—or vision, if he were to name it true—he had been inside her mind and had felt the perverse joy she had known with every act against God and man that she had committed.

Sam squatted over her, his knees steeped in the snow, and he raised the black iron peg over his head, grasped in both hands. It trembled as he trembled, the way the blade must have shaken in old Abraham's hands in the days of yore, certain in his righteous obedience to God but torn in half by his own conscience.

"You," he growled through hot, unbidden tears at the still form that lay below him in the snow, "are not Lucy anymore."

"Samuel," he heard Charlotte say, not so much a word as it was a musical note from the angels on high. A pluck of celestial harps saving him from this terrible deed.

He turned to see the woman standing in the doorway of the house. She held onto the wooden threshold to steady herself and she was bent over like an old woman. Her other hand clutched at her bandaged midsection tenderly.

"Don't, Samuel," she said, grimacing. "She's still my daughter."

Sam shook his head, glanced back to the girl.

"She'll never be your daughter again, Charlotte. Could be she never was."

"I'll let the priest and the doctors decide on that," she said. "That's my burden to bear, not yours."

Do it, boy, he heard the voice of his father in his head. *Cave the devil-child's skull in!*

He didn't want his father to be right, but he was. The old man had always been right. Sam could end it here, end it tonight and walk away from this fallen house and all its fallen souls, never to return.

It'll never be over, though, he thought as he looked up, searching the dark tree line of the forest.

The Wasp King was still out there somewhere, mad and roaming the wilds. An old man like him wouldn't last another night—if he had lasted the first. But Horace and Lucy were vessels for Mammon, the devil of Evermore, and that creature could bend nature to its will.

Sam wiped the wet from his eyes and sighed, his breath a ghostly fog in the night.

Lucy could die tonight or she could live, he realized, and it would make no difference. If he bashed her head in, the only difference would be the blood on his own hands. And there had been more than enough blood spilled on account of this place.

He stood and tossed Colvin's iron peg back onto the porch, leaned down and scooped the unconscious girl up. With Lucy laid over his shoulder like a bag of horse oats, he stepped into the house again.

"Lay her on the bed, Sam," Charlotte said. "In my room."

After setting Lucy on her mother's bed, Sam went back into the ruin of the girl's bedroom to collect his missing weapon. Minutes later, he and Charlotte sat by the bedside. She had brought a blanket in with her and she cradled it on her lap. He wasn't sure if it was for her or for the girl sleeping on the bed.

In the flickering lamp light, Lucy looked peaceful, serene. The picture of a sweet child dreaming of carefree days, of birds and butterflies, flowers and lace dresses.

Hell, he thought, *maybe she's having just that sort of dream.*

Maybe when she was asleep, the demon inside of her slept, too. For her sake, Sam hoped it was true.

"It'll be light soon," Sam said, getting to his feet. "I should get old Cutter ready to travel."

Charlotte wiped at a tear rolling from her eye.

"Will you take her?"

Sam nodded. "She'll need to come with me. To Selburn. I'll lock her up first, then call on Doc Blanchard to examine her, make sure she's...all right, I guess."

"And then?"

"You can bring in the priest or whatever doctors you want. Maybe it'll help," he said, lowering his gaze from Charlotte's piercing stare. "No matter what, though, I'm going to charge her with murder, Charlotte."

It was Charlotte's turn to look away.

"I understand," she said.

He turned to leave and got only a few steps before she spoke again.

"You don't think they can help her, do you?" she asked. "Not the priest, not the doctors."

He sighed. "Don't see how what I think matters, Charlotte," he said. "But since you ask, what I think is that they never could have. The devil went to Lucy because it saw something of itself in her. That's what I think."

The best thing for Lucy, he thought, awfully, *would've been a stillbirth. Best thing for baby Nathan, for William, for Mary, for everyone.*

He glanced back at her, ashamed of the thought, but knowing it was true nonetheless.

"Thank you, Sam," Charlotte said, going to the bed and sitting next to Lucy, the folded blanket tucked under her arm.

He tipped his hat and left the room.

Walking down the hall, he felt dead on his feet. The last thing he had the inclination to do was ride to Selburn with that evil girl shackled to him. Sam got to the balcony that looked down onto the foyer. Below, Seena was comforting Twig. Bet—now bandaged up and moving slowly, with a swath of cloth covering his damaged eye and wrapped around his head—was helping Colvin rig his leg back on. The grandfather clock tolled the hour as Sam cast about the cavernous old manor house.

Everything about this place was cold and he wondered if love had ever lived here. For all its finery and comforts, he found it hard to believe Evermore had felt like a home to any of them. It was dark and impersonal, the objects collected in it like props in a stage play. Even the patriarch's storied past, he thought—glancing over to the wall of war memorabilia outside the master's chambers—seemed as if it belonged to another man.

Sam's eye caught on something. Or, rather, a lack of something.

Beneath the map of Mexico, two empty hooks jutted out from the polished oak wall. His fatigued mind dwelled on it a moment before it all came together.

Horace Crownhill's Colt pistol was missing.

Sam recalled the blanket Charlotte had brought into the bedroom with her, never unfolding, strangely clutching to it like a child.

"Charlotte!" he called out and turned back down the hallway.

Sam got no farther than two steps before the shot rang out. He drew his own pistol—more out of habit than anything—and continued down the hall with caution.

Through the open door of her bedroom, Sam could see Charlotte seated on the bed, cradling her daughter's lifeless body in her arms. A red stain spread across the back of Lucy's nightgown where the bullet blasted through her chest and out the other side. Charlotte had set the gun on the bedside table and now held her daughter close, bawling into the curve of her daughter's lolling neck, rocking back and forth as if lulling her baby girl to sleep.

Damn it all, Sam thought, closing his eyes and turning away.

He could not wait to be rid of this place—to be rid of its madness, its perpetual death, and the black secrets the family kept, poisoning them all. He would return to Selburn in defeat, it would seem. Although, despite his feeling that he had failed fair Charlotte in serving or protecting anyone, another part of him knew that he never stood a chance, that he had been too late the very moment he arrived. The old slaves with their stories had been so right—this family had been lost long ago, claimed by the malevolence of the land itself, as had been so many who came before them.

Sam descended the stairway. Charlotte's anguished moans poured down from above, echoing among the high walls of the foyer. Colvin and the others were gathered there, watching him amble down the stairs, their faces stricken and woeful. The trembling old woman leaned on her younger kinfolk and looked so weak and in such poor health that he wondered if she would even last the night.

Another gunshot pierced the quiet gloom and Charlotte Crownhill wept no more.

Sam stopped only a moment, for he had known that shot would come as surely as the clock in the hall would strike the next hour. He also knew that it must have torn Charlotte's heart into shreds to bring death to her only daughter, even if it had to be done. Too much blood had been spilled, too many tears shed.

He reckoned that the moment she pulled the trigger, Charlotte knew that she would follow Lucy into the grave. Right there in the same chamber the girl had very likely been born in.

Sheriff Sam Lock did not pause for a goodbye as he walked past the long faces in the foyer and out of the house into the chill darkness of the night. He offered no consoling words, no damning accusations. He spoke no words at all, in fact. He only gritted his teeth against his trembling lips and closed his eyes as a single tear rolled forth and down his face, its acid touch like the sting of a wasp.

CHAPTER 14
A DARK RECOUNTING

The sun was breaking over the horizon when the sheriff returned to his home in Selburn. He retired to his bedroom with the intention of sleeping for a few hours. Instead, he lay there in the soft light of the dawning morning, unable to keep his eyes closed.

Every time he shut them against the creeping daylight, Charlotte was waiting for him. Some brief flash of memory—the first time he had laid eyes on her and her easy smile, which he had not gotten to see nearly often enough. The curve and shade of her bare, milky skin when they were together that night. The breathless shudder of her body. These images were difficult for him to bear, but they were not the only specters that came to him. The many horrors he had seen at Evermore marched through the darkness behind his eyelids in a weird parade, irrepressible and ceaseless.

For all the fine things and wealthy affectations the Crownhills possessed, it had not been enough to save them. In fact, he realized, it had damned them. Damned them all. Perhaps, though, they were fundamentally blameless in their fate. That land had been fought for and murdered upon for a long time before the Crownhills laid the cornerstone of Evermore. Once the house had been built, there had been no other destiny for it and all those within its walls. They might as well have built the estate on the soft earth of a swamp. There would never be anything but ruin there.

The land and the malevolent thing that dwelled there swallowed them whole in the end. No amount of money could have bought them out of that dark fate.

And no lawman could have stopped it either.

This is what Sam told himself. Over and over again, he told it, hoping it would catch and he would start believing it. But just as the memories were still too fresh to be disappeared from his attempts at sleep, the psychic wounds he had suffered in that old house had not yet been divested of their venom. Likely, they would not for some time to come. He wondered how many nights he would lay in the dark to find rest and the phantoms of Evermore would come, baring tooth and claw.

How long before their edge would be dulled?

Unwilling to indulge a futile effort, Sam rose from the bed and set about getting a kettle of hot water going for a hot bath. He would pick up where he had begun. It was the only way to move forward past the terror and death and the things beyond explanation.

Just do your job, he thought to himself. *Protect the weak, punish the wicked and go home at night. Get up in every morning, put one foot in front of the other and keep doing your job.*

After a brief and ultimately unsatisfying soak in the bath, Sam dressed and left the house. He led Cutter down to the Sheriff's Office where he collected Deputy Smyth and a few other rough but dutiful men that he trusted well enough and together they began the trip back to the Crownhill estate by way of the regular road. Sam would not again set foot in the woods between the town and Evermore, considering them a blight upon the land, where something infinitely darker than the family's secrets held sway.

The sheriff told his deputy only that the Crownhills were deeply troubled folk and that murder had been done there, right under his nose, after which Charlotte Crownhill had taken her own life.

The men rounded a bend in the road. Snow-capped columns of mountain rock flanked the entrance road that wound around the glen to the house. The soft stone tablets embedded in those columns that bore the estate's name had been vandalized—a crude "N" scratched into being before the first engraved "E".

NEvermore.

Bemused by what must have been the handiwork of Colvin or his nephews, Sam then caught the scent of a smoldering fire drifting through the air. Every man that rode with him past those columns knew what they would find even though it would be another mile or so before they beheld the black husk of Evermore with their own eyes.

Sam sent Smyth and the others out into the nearby woods to search for any sign of Horace. It was likely a fool's errand and Sam knew it. If the Wasp King was out there now, he was either dead and had been reclaimed by the accursed land or he was holding court on his gnarled and twisted throne somewhere in between this world and the next, a ghastly spirit to be whispered about for generations to come. Either way, he hoped his men would find nothing.

Sam rode Cutter up to what was left of the front steps of the house. There he found the old woman, Seena picking among the rubble for anything of the family's that might be salvaged. She didn't look surprised to see him.

"The lone survivor, huh?" he called out to her.

She snorted. "If you can call it survivin'."

At the edge of the wood north of the property, Sam glimpsed four freshly disturbed patches of earth—dark spots in the snow that could only be graves for those who had fallen during his time at Evermore.

"And the others?"

Seena saw his gaze clinging to the graves and sighed.

"We put 'em to rest, Sheriff," she said. "Then Colvin and the boys cleared out. Said he was takin' your advice and headin' north."

"Was it Colvin that burned the house? Just like he burned your quarters that night?"

She chewed over the question.

"I ain't looking to arrest anyone, don't worry," he said. "Far as I'm concerned it was the best thing for the place."

She threw her head back and laughed.

"Reckon you and me in agreement on that count, Sheriff."

He watched her picking through the blackened stone and timber. Making her way through it, she bent over and plucked a brass button from the wreck, shined it against her skirt and tossed it to him.

It was so warm in his hand that he could barely hold it.

"It was Miss Charlotte's, you know," she said. "Figured you might want somethin' to keep."

He swallowed down a lump in his throat.

"Why would you think that?"

She straightened—as much as the hunched old woman *could* straighten—and gave him a scornful look. "I seen the way you two was when y'all was together, boy. I may be old but I ain't stupid."

He looked down at the shiny brass thing, a button from one of her dresses, no doubt. Perhaps even one that he had seen her in.

"Well, thank you," he said as he dropped it into the pocket of his duster.

The old woman paid him no mind, just returned to her gathering. Out of the corner of his eye, he saw his men returning from their errand, thankful that they appeared empty-handed.

"Seena," Sam asked, "what is it you're doing exactly?"

"Collectin' the story, child. What else would I be doin'?"

Sam cocked his head, confused.

"The story?"

"Why, sure," she said, turning to him. "Every house got a family, Sheriff. And every family got a story. It's writ in the ash and bones of whatever's left when they're gone. Some stories is worth tellin'. Some ain't."

He considered it, bemused.

"And the story of the Crownhills?" he asked.

She fixed him with a solemn look and shook her head.

He supposed she was right. What worth was there in such a tale of malice and death? It wouldn't even serve as a proper parable to warn someone away. There was no accounting for the diabolic force that had set its wrath upon the family and no way it might have been avoided.

Seena's right, Sam thought. There was no lesson to be learned here. There was only a dark recounting.

"Sheriff?"

Sam turned to see Deputy Smyth and his men pulling their horses alongside of him.

"Didn't find anything?" he asked the young man.

"No, sir. Not a thing."

He nodded.

"Sheriff," Smyth prodded him, "who were you talking to?"

"Well, I was..." he turned to point in Seena's direction but saw now that she was not there. Perhaps she never had been.

"No one,..."

Sam climbed back onto his horse and took one last look at what remained of the once-grand Crownhill estate. When he rode away that afternoon, he aimed to never again return. He would go back to Selburn, to his own modest home, and pour another hot bath in hopes that this one would wash away the harrowing events of the past few days.

A cool wind blew across the hill and the men stiffened their collars in its wake. The sheriff thought of Seena's words and wondered if seeing her had been nothing more than some fantasy his mind had concocted, an attempt to find reason amidst the senseless tragedy. Although, when he shoved his hand into his coat pocket, he pulled forth the brass button and, opening his palm, stared at it for a moment—still warm and plenty real.

"What you got there, Sheriff?" the deputy inquired, leaning out of his saddle for a better look.

"Nothing," he whispered, closing the button in his fist.

Sam smiled bitterly, recalling the taste of rosewater on Charlotte's perfumed skin, now a secret of his own to keep.

ACKNOWLEDGMENTS

My sincerest thanks to a few people who helped me shape this book into its final form. Richard Thomas, Robert S. Wilson, Doug Murano, and Sydney Leigh. A special thanks to the late David G. Barnett. To Erik Wilson for the original cover art and to François Vaillancourt for the current cover artwork.

ABOUT THE AUTHOR

D. ALEXANDER WARD is an author and anthologist of horror and dark fiction. He is the author of numerous short stories and the novels Beneath Ash & Bone and Blood Savages.

As an anthologist, he edited the Bram Stoker Award-nominated anthologies Lost Highways: Dark Fictions From the Road and GUTTED: Beautiful Horror Stories (co-edited) from Crystal Lake publishing as well as the anthologies The Seven Deadliest and Shadows Over Main Street, Volumes 1 and 2 (co-edited).

He is an Active Member of the Horror Writers Association and very involved in the small press publishing world of horror and dark fiction. His online footprints can be found everywhere and he can regularly be spotted on various and sundry social media outlets.

Along with his beloved wife and daughter and the haints in the woods, he lives near the farm where he grew up in what used to be rural Virginia, where his love for the people, passions, and folklore of the South was nurtured. There, he spends his nights penning and collecting tales of the dark, strange, and fantastic.

www.ingramcontent.com/pod-product-compliance
Lightning Source LLC
LaVergne TN
LVHW092049060526
838201LV00047B/1304